DOUBLE CROSSED!

The Case of the Missing Money

HILDA STAHL

Accent Books™ is an imprint of David C. Cook Publishing Co.
David C. Cook Publishing Co., Elgin, Illinois 60120
David C. Cook Publishing Co., Weston, Ontario
Nova Distribution Ltd., Newton Abbot, England

DOUBLE CROSSED!

Revised 1993

Cover design and illustration by Terry Julien
First Printing, 1987
Printed in the United States of America
97 96 95 94 93 7 6 5 4 3

Library of Congress Catalog Card Number 86-72124

ISBN 0-7814-0524-6

CONTENTS

1

THE FIGHT

Before she could stop herself, Wren grabbed Paula's arm and swung her around hard. Fire shot from Wren's dark eyes. The cold October wind whipped her long hair back. "I just heard what you did, Paula Gantz!"

The color drained from Paula's face. "What did I do?"

Wren could barely speak. "Bobby just told me!"

"So?" Paula tried to break free, but Wren's grip tightened.

"He says the whole school knows by now." Wren's voice broke, and a fresh wave of anger washed through her. She glanced at Bess beside her, then back to Paula.

"Let her go, Wren," Bess whispered weakly.

Paula wet her lips with the tip of her tongue. "I don't know what you're talking about, Wren."

Wren clenched her teeth and glared at Paula. "You know all right. And you know you weren't supposed to tell. Miss Brewster said it was to be kept between the few of us who knew."

"I don't care!" Paula's voice rang out and Wren shot a look around to see if any of the other students had heard. Thankfully no one seemed to notice.

Wren pushed her face close to Paula's and said in a hoarse whisper, "How dare you tell everyone my secret, Paula?"

Paula jerked free and glared at Wren. "I can do anything I want, Wren House! So there!"

"Don't fight with her, Wren," begged Bess, her blue eyes wide and her face pale. She tugged at Wren's arm. "I'm your very best friend, and I must stop you! You don't want to get in trouble with Miss Brewster for fighting in the school yard."

Wren turned an angry frown at Bess, and Bess backed away. An icy band tightened around Wren's heart. She didn't want to fight with anyone, but Paula had embarrassed her in front of the entire fifth grade at Jordan Christian Academy. "Stay out of this, Bess. It's between Paula and me."

"But you can't fight with her, Wren." Bess pushed her hands down into her jacket pockets. "Jesus doesn't want you to. Nobody wants you to. You don't even want to."

"Better listen to her," snapped Paula. "You're already in enough trouble with all your dumb detective work." Paula raised her voice. "And with the story you made up for the school newspaper."

Wren's face turned as bright red as her sweater. "I

already said I was sorry for that story. Miss Brewster said we were to keep quiet about it. Miss Brewster labeled it fiction. Besides, I handed in another one and you know it. You're just jealous because I wrote a better story than you did."

"Me?" Paula tapped her chest. "Me, jealous? Jealous of a Bird House? Never!"

Bess reached for Wren. "Let's go inside. The bell just rang and it's time to go in."

Wren ignored Bess and faced Paula squarely. "I told you not to call me Bird House or Bird Nest again!"

"I'll call you anything I want!"

"My name is Wren Lorrene House."

Paula narrowed her eyes. "Bird House!"

Just then three boys ran past and bumped against Paula, sending her sprawling against Wren. The girls fell to the ground with a thud. Wren shoved against Paula and Paula pushed back. Bess grabbed at Wren's arm, but missed.

Just then Wren saw huge, Nike-covered feet just inches from her face. She glanced up, up, and up until she met dark eyes scowling down at her. Her heart thudded painfully. "Hello, Mr. Abram," she whispered hoarsely.

"What's going on here?" asked Mr. Abram.

"It's all Wren's fault!" cried Paula.

"It is not!"

Mr. Abram stood over the girls, a scowl on his face. He

gripped Wren's arm with one hand and Paula's with the other. "You girls know it's against the rules to fight. I'm surprised at both of you."

"They weren't fighting," said Bess, her trembling hands pressed tightly together.

Mr. Abram gave Bess a stern look. "Lying is not tolerated at JCA either."

"Me? Lie?" Tears sprang to Bess's eyes. "I don't lie. Do I, Wren?"

"No. No, you don't," Wren said softly. She brushed dirt off her leg and the hem of her skirt. "Mr. Abram, Bess does not lie. Paula and I were arguing, not fighting."

"She started it," said Paula, jabbing a finger at Wren.

Mr. Abram pointed toward the brick building. "I don't have time to settle this. You'll have to report to the office and let Mr. Gozzie handle it."

Wren bit back an argument. She could see from the look on Paula's face that she wanted to say something too.

Bess blinked back tears and darted a look around. The other students were already inside the school. Wren knew Bess would be humiliated if Neil saw her walk to the office in disgrace.

"Go right to the office, girls," said Mr. Abram. "I have a gym class now and I'm trusting you to obey me. I'll call Mr. Gozzie from my class."

As soon as he disappeared into his classroom, Paula

whispered, "Let's go. He won't really call Mr. Gozzie."

Bess moved restlessly. "I wish we could go home right now."

"We have to go to the office," said Wren.

Paula made a face as Bess agreed reluctantly, "You're right."

A few minutes later Wren took a deep breath and knocked on the principal's office door. She glanced back as Bess sniffed and knuckled away tears. "Mr. Gozzie will know we weren't fighting. He won't yell at us."

"He'll call our parents," whispered Bess.

Paula gasped and shook her head. "No! He can't! I don't want him to."

"Why not?" asked Wren. "You won't get spanked or anything. You never get spanked or yelled at or punished. You always get everything you want no matter what it is."

"You're spoiled," agreed Bess.

Paula trembled. "I am not!"

"Yes, you are." Bess nodded hard, and looked as if she would have said more, but just then the office door opened. Mr. Gozzie stood there with his jacket open and his tie firmly knotted around the collar of his white shirt. "Come in, girls. Mr. Abram tells me that you were fighting outdoors. What do you have to say for yourselves?"

"We weren't fighting," all three said at once.

"That's not what I heard. Please sit down."

"We weren't fighting," they all said again as they

walked slowly into the office and perched uneasily on the edge of their chairs.

Mr. Gozzie picked a twig out of Wren's hair and motioned to the dirt on Paula's jacket. "Then how did that happen?"

"We were pushed down," said Wren.

Mr. Gozzie shook his head. "Mr. Abram says he saw only you three." He looked down at them with a sad look in his eyes. "I'll have to call your parents."

"No!" the girls cried in one voice.

"Please, don't," said Wren, looking up at Mr. Gozzie with her most pleading look. She tried to sort out her argument just the way her mom did when she was going to court with a client.

"We were arguing and some boys ran past and knocked us down on top of each other. We weren't fighting. If you tell our parents that we were, we'll be punished. Punished unjustly." Wren lifted her chin. She liked the sound of her argument. "And if we're punished, we might not be able to put on the program that we're supposed to put on for being the class that sold the most subscriptions to the *Good News Weekly.*"

"That's right," said Bess.

"Wren's mother is a lawyer," said Paula. "She taught Wren how to argue a case."

Wren shot Paula a look that should have closed her mouth, but it didn't.

"Her mother might even sue you for harassment."

Wren rolled her eyes. She knew Paula had probably heard the word on TV and wanted to sound important.

Mr. Gozzie flipped back his jacket and stood with his hands resting on his hips. "Girls, don't make more trouble for yourselves." He walked around his desk and sat down in a large leather chair.

Wren sank back on the yellow plastic chair and locked her hands together in her lap. A fresh argument whirled around inside her head, but she didn't want to use it in case it made Mr. Gozzie more upset than he was already. With a sinking heart, she watched him pick up the phone to call.

Paula sat on her hands and swallowed hard. "My dad's at his office or at the hospital delivering a baby, and my mom had some meetings to go to this morning. You won't be able to talk to them now."

Bess frowned thoughtfully. "My mom might be home, but my dad won't be."

"My mom's in court today," said Wren. "And if my dad's at home, he'll probably be with a client. He's a detective, you know."

Mr. Gozzie kept the phone to his ear. "There's no answer at your house, Wren." He tried the Gantz home and then the Talbot home. "No answer. I'll send notes homes with you girls for your parents. Please ask them to call me."

"But we weren't fighting!" cried Paula. "Honest!"

"We weren't," said Bess just above a whisper.

"It only looked like it," said Wren. "May I explain again what happened?"

Mr. Gozzie fingered a yellow pencil for a minute, then nodded.

Wren took a deep breath. "Please keep an open mind while I explain. You don't want to judge the incident on appearance only."

Mr. Gozzie's lips twitched and Wren thought he was going to laugh, but instead, he cleared his throat and said, "Continue, please."

Wren stood up before him in the way that she'd seen her mom do it in court. "Mr. Gozzie, Paula and I were arguing over something personal. It was a heated argument, but we didn't hit each other."

Mr. Gozzie chuckled, but quickly covered it with a cough.

"During the heated discussion between Paula and myself, three boys ran past and bumped into us. I don't know if it was accidental or if it was planned. They knocked us down to the ground in a heap and that's when Mr. Abram came along. He honestly thought we were having a fight, but we weren't. And that's the whole truth, so help me God."

With a serious look on her face Wren lifted her hand up, palm out. "Now that you've heard the details, may we please be dismissed and sent to our class?"

Mr. Gozzie stood up. "Wren, you'd make a fine lawyer."

"Thank you, sir, but I'm a detective like my dad."

"She's always wanted to be a detective," said Paula.

Bess just covered her face and groaned.

Mr. Gozzie walked around the desk. "Girls, I believe your story. I'll write an excused tardy for you." He scratched on a pad with a ballpoint pen, then handed the folded note to Wren. "You may go to your class. I won't call your parents."

"Thank you!" they said together.

"Hurry to class now," said Mr. Gozzie, opening the door for them.

Her eyes sparkling, Wren turned to Bess and Paula. Their eyes were alight with relief. Together they walked out of the principal's office.

2

PLANS

Wren stopped outside the fifth-grade room and turned to Bess and Paula. "Don't embarrass us by telling that we were sent to the office for fighting."

"I won't!" Bess touched her flushed cheeks. "Never!"

"Why should I tell anyone?" asked Paula with a shrug.

Wren breathed easier. She didn't want to be teased about being sent to the office, but most of all she didn't want Brian Davies to find out about it.

Her hand trembled as she reached for the door. She stopped with her hand on the doorknob. She thought about her anger toward Paula, and she knew that the Lord wanted her to forgive Paula for telling everyone about what she'd done.

"What's wrong, Wren?" asked Bess. "We have to go into class."

"I know." But still she didn't move.

"Will you move and let me open the door?" Paula jabbed Wren in the back. "I don't want any more trouble."

Wren took a deep breath. She knew it was now or never. "Paula, I'm sorry for getting mad at you and yelling at you."

Paula's mouth dropped open.

"I forgive you for telling my secret," said Wren.

Paula rolled her eyes and shook her head. "You're crazy."

Wren glanced at Bess, and Bess smiled knowingly. Wren turned back to Paula. Even if Paula thought she was crazy, Wren knew she had done what was right.

With a light heart she opened the door and stepped inside the room with Bess and Paula. Miss Brewster stopped reading the Bible passage and looked at them.

"Come in, girls."

"We have a pass from Mr. Gozzic," said Wren. She handed it to Miss Brewster, then turned and walked to her seat. She wouldn't meet Tim's eyes in case he read her thoughts and asked an embarrassing question. Last year she hadn't liked Tim Avery. But this year she'd learned that he liked a mystery as much as she did, and they had become good friends.

She folded her hands on her desk and listened while Miss Brewster finished the Bible reading for the day.

An hour later, just after English class, Miss Brewster said, "We have to finish our plans for the program that we're giving for the friends and families who have helped us make money to buy our copy machine. Paula, do you have an update report on subscriptions to the *Good News Weekly?*"

Paula pulled out her three-ring binder and opened it with a flourish. "We now have eighty subscriptions to the paper. At five dollars a year each, that comes to $400. I myself found ten subscribers." She looked around as if she expected everyone to applaud. No one did. Wren sat very still and tried not to frown.

"That is wonderful, Paula." Miss Brewster walked across the front of the room. Her skirt swirled around her long legs. The pleasant aroma of her perfume reached Wren. "Did you remember to turn the money bag in to the office?"

"Oh, yes. I never forget that." Paula shot a sharp look around the room at the other students. "Remember, tomorrow is the last day to hand in money. Find people after school who want to buy our paper and bring the money in the morning."

"You've all worked hard on this project," said Miss Brewster. "And I'm proud of you. The school contest we had is over and our class won, but we don't want to stop trying to sell subscriptions. Keep selling. There are still many people interested in the newspaper, and I know you'll be able to find them."

Paula waved her arm high.

"Yes, Paula."

"Don't forget that I get to sing for the program."

Wren slid low in her seat and doubled her fists into tight balls. Before Paula came to JCA, she was the one always chosen to sing. Now she always had to share time with Paula, or Paula got to sing because she volunteered first and Wren had to do something else. It just wasn't fair!

Mom and Dad had said that Wren should ask God to help her be patient. Just last night her mom had said, "Remember, Wren, God has given you a special singing talent. He will help you find opportunities to use your voice for Him. Just ask the Lord to show you the opportunities so that you can step into them and perform—for His glory." Wren had prayed and deep down she knew that God was watching over her—even if it looked like Paula was getting all the breaks.

Miss Brewster nodded. "Yes, Paula, you do get to sing. You have a beautiful voice, and we're all looking forward to hearing you again."

Wren bit her lower lip. She wasn't looking forward to hearing Paula.

Paula looked very smug, and Wren turned away from her before she said something bad to her.

Miss Brewster pulled out her clipboard. "Joyce, Tina, and David will do the skit we chose. Russ and Sean will sing a duet. Jason, Levi, and Tim will do the puppet show."

Wren smiled at Tim, and he smiled back. She knew he

liked working with the puppets. She would've liked working them with him, but she'd been given a poem to read instead. She listened halfheartedly as Miss Brewster finished reading the program.

"One last thing," said Miss Brewster. She smiled as if she was pleased about something. "Last night three different people called me to request that Wren sing at the program."

With a gasp Wren sat up straight.

"I told them that we didn't want the program to seem like a songfest, but they said one song from you would make the program extra special. I told them that I'd ask you, Wren. Will you sing?"

Wren's eyes widened and her heart leapt for joy. God had answered!

"Yes! Yes, I'll sing!"

"Good. We all enjoy your singing, Wren."

Out of the corner of her eye, Wren saw Paula make a face, but she ignored her.

Miss Brewster wrote on the yellow paper clipped to the board. "Wren, you tell me what song you'd like to sing, and we'll discuss it tomorrow."

Wren nodded. "I will. I'll ask my mom and she'll help me find the right song for the program."

"Good," said Miss Brewster.

"I don't think that's fair," said Paula with a pout. "I should be the only one to sing."

"You and Wren will both sing," said Miss Brewster. "It'll make our program twice as nice."

Paula snorted, but didn't argue further.

Wren smiled and thought about all the songs she knew. It was hard to keep her mind on schoolwork for the rest of the day.

After school Tim stopped her with a shout. She walked to the bike stand where he always locked his ten-speed.

"Hi," she said with a smile.

He grinned and his freckles seemed to stretch across his face. "I think Amos Pike was one of the people who called to ask for you to sing in the program."

Wren laughed. "Good old Amos Pike." They had first met him in September when they were working on their school movie assignment and they'd been good friends since. He was like a grandfather to them and they liked visiting him as often as they could.

Paula pushed in between Tim and Wren. "I heard that! I'm going to tell Miss Brewster that you paid Amos Pike to call her!"

"I did not!" cried Wren. "Don't you say that I did!"

Paula glared at Wren. "You'd do anything to get to sing. You love to show off in front of everybody."

"Me?" Wren sputtered as she doubled her fists and clenched her teeth. How she wanted to punch Paula right in the nose! Silently she asked God to help her be patient and kind.

"Leave Wren alone, Paula," said Tim. "She doesn't know who called Miss Brewster and neither do I. I just said that maybe Amos Pike called."

Paula tossed her head. "Well, I bet he did call. If I find out that you made him call, I'll tell Miss Brewster. I'll tell the whole school, and you won't get to sing. So there!"

Wren shrugged. "Good-bye, Paula. See you tomorrow."

Paula frowned and looked around. "Are you going somewhere?"

"No, you are," said Tim. "You're leaving. Wren and I want to talk."

Paula pushed her hands hard into her jacket pockets. "You hate me, don't you? I know you do."

Wren sighed. "We don't hate you, Paula."

"Yes, you do. Everybody does. But I don't care! So there!" Paula spun on her heels and ran down the sidewalk. Suddenly she stopped and turned back. "Wren loves Tim. Wren loves Tim!" she chanted at the top of her lungs.

Just then Brian Davies walked past and glanced toward Wren and Tim. "Wren loves Tim!" Paula chanted again, then laughed and ran away.

Wren's cheeks flushed bright red, and a sick feeling rose inside of her. How dare Paula chant that right in front of Brian Davies? Wren groaned and slowly walked away from Tim and toward home.

3

MISSING MONEY

Wren glanced around the room as she sank to her desk. It seemed like everyone was watching her, remembering what Paula had chanted yesterday. Wren scowled at Paula's back.

Miss Brewster walked from her desk to the window beside it. She turned, and the morning sun shining through the window glinted on her head and shoulders. "Class, yesterday we discussed our theme for the program we're putting on for the community. For those of you who missed our discussion, we decided to use the theme 'Rejoice in the Lord.' " Miss Brewster looked right at Wren, and Wren sank lower at her desk. She had missed that discussion while she, Bess, and Paula had been in the office. Finally Miss Brewster smiled, then looked away, and Wren could breathe easier.

"We'll have recitations, puppets, music, and a short skit. The program will last an hour. Admission will be charged, and the money will go toward our new copy machine along with the money from our newspaper subscriptions." Miss Brewster walked back to her desk. Her skirt swayed against her slender legs. Her blue sweater matched her eyes. "Paula, please bring me the subscription money that you brought from the office a while ago."

Paula's head shot up. "I already gave you the money, Miss Brewster. You put it in your second desk drawer."

Wren leaned forward, suddenly alert. Was there a mystery to solve? If she had a mystery to solve, she might be able to forget that Brian Davies had heard Paula chant, "Wren loves Tim."

Miss Brewster pushed back her hair and frowned slightly. "Paula, I just looked and it's not there. I thought you might have needed it again for your records." The class buzzed with whispers, but she silenced them with a finger to her lips. "Paula, are you sure you don't have it?"

"I'm positive. I'll look in your drawer. Maybe it got pushed way to the back." Paula ran to the desk and opened the second drawer. "Here's a pad of paper, three pencils, and your purse." She paused as the color drained from her face. "But the bank bag with the checks and cash is gone!" She shivered and Wren thought she was going to faint right in front of the entire class. Slowly she turned to face Miss Brewster. "The bag is gone. The money is gone."

Wren had to grip her seat to keep from leaping up to say, "I'll solve the mystery! I'll find the bag!"

Miss Brewster patted Paula's shoulder. "Paula, don't get upset. I'm sure it has to be in the room somewhere. I saw you with it at your desk a while ago."

"But that was just after I came back from the office with it. Kris gave me her three checks and I had to enter them in my book. Then I put the bag in your desk." Paula shot a look around the room. "Did anyone see the bag? Did one of you take it to play a mean trick on me? Give it back right now!"

Wren studied the faces around her for a hint of guilt. No one looked guilty. The buzz of voices rose until several of the children were shouting.

Miss Brewster held up her hand, but the talking continued. "Quiet, please! This is serious. There was a lot of money in that bag. This is not the time to play a prank. We need the money back now."

Wren's heart jerked. Who took the money? She wanted to jump up to look for clues.

"Is somebody playing a dumb joke on me?" asked Paula. "Are you, Jim?"

"Me? I didn't do it!" Jim flushed and ducked his head.

"Levi?"

"Never! I don't play practical jokes."

Paula turned from Levi and pointed at Wren. "Or maybe you want to get even with me, Wren. Maybe you took the money."

"I did not!" cried Wren. Didn't they know she was a

detective and not a criminal?

Paula narrowed her eyes. "You look very guilty."

Wren sat up very straight. "Well, I'm not guilty!"

"I think you are!"

"Girls," said Miss Brewster in a warning voice.

Wren pointed her finger at Paula. "I think you took it just to blame me for it."

"No! Don't say that!" Paula whirled around to Miss Brewster. "That's not true at all! I don't know where the money is."

Miss Brewster patted Paula's shoulder. "I'm not blaming you, Paula."

Paula pressed her hands to her head. "This is just awful. What am I going to do now?"

"Calm down, Paula. I'm sure the money is here." Miss Brewster reached for another desk drawer. "It must be in a different drawer. Or maybe even in your desk, Paula. You look in your desk, and I'll look in mine."

"It's not in my desk," said Paula, but she marched to her desk and peered inside.

Wren waited, her heart thudding against her rib cage. Excitement bubbled up inside her, and she could barely sit still. Maybe a new mystery was unfolding right in the fifth-grade classroom at JCA. A few days ago she'd solved a mystery, and she was ready to begin another one now.

Paula searched her desk. "I told you it wouldn't be here," she cried as she turned to Miss Brewster in panic.

Miss Brewster sank to her desk. She rubbed a hand over her cheek. "The money is gone. This is serious, boys and girls. Is someone playing a trick on Paula or on me? Please. I must know. Now."

Wren wriggled, unable to sit still a second longer. There was a mystery to solve right under her nose. She smiled excitedly.

Paula saw Wren's smile, and she stamped her foot and stuck her finger almost in Wren's face. "You took the money! Didn't you, Wren House? You want to get even with me for what I did to you!"

"I did not!" Wren cried.

Miss Brewster studied Wren thoughtfully. "Wren, did you take the money?"

"No!" Wren shook her head hard. Her dark hair swished back and forth. "I would never do such a terrible thing!"

Miss Brewster was quiet a long time, and Wren knew she was thinking about her false newspaper story. "I'd hate to think that you would do it."

"I wouldn't take the money, Miss Brewster," Wren said with a break in her voice. "I know I lied about the story, but I made that right. I would never steal." She looked around at the whispering students and caught the look of sympathy on Tim's face. He smiled at her and she felt a little better. "Please believe me, Miss Brewster. I know I did something wrong before, but I wouldn't do anything as terrible as stealing money."

"She wouldn't," said Bess.

"That's right," said Tim.

"How about you, Bess?" asked Paula sharply.

Bess gasped. "Me? I would never steal! Never!"

"Tim?" asked Paula sharply. "I know you hate me."

Tim frowned. "I don't hate you, and I didn't take the money."

"Then who did?" demanded Paula.

"Yes, who?" asked several children at once.

"It's a true mystery," whispered Wren, feeling pleased.

Tim raised his hand. His red hair stuck on end. His freckles stood out boldly on his skin.

"Yes, Tim," said Miss Brewster.

"I think Paula took the money herself just to make trouble for the class."

Several others agreed.

"I did not!" cried Paula, jumping up. "I didn't!"

"Quiet everyone," said Miss Brewster. "This isn't getting us anywhere."

"I didn't take the money," said Paula hoarsely. "Doesn't anyone believe me?"

Wren could tell that some of the students didn't believe Paula. Maybe even Miss Brewster didn't believe Paula. Wren grinned. Then guilt rose inside her and she squirmed uneasily.

"I'll call Mr. Gozzie and he'll advise us on what to do," said Miss Brewster.

"Call the police," said Paula. "They'll find the thief."

"Handcuffs for Paula," said one of the boys in the back of the room. Several students laughed as Paula flushed.

Wren folded her hands on her desk and listened to Miss Brewster quiet the room again. Wren thought about Paula and the money. Paula didn't need to steal to have all the money she wanted. If she had taken the money, it was for another reason. Wren narrowed her eyes thoughtfully. If she knew the motive, the crime would be easier to solve. Maybe she should ask Miss Brewster to put her on the case. Wren shook her head. Miss Brewster didn't think she was a very good detective. Miss Brewster would probably tell her to let the adults solve it.

Tim waved his hand in the air again.

"Yes, Tim." Miss Brewster sounded very tired.

"Wren and I will solve the case of the missing money."

"We will," said Wren. She wanted to jump up and pat Tim on the back, but she stayed in her desk and tried to act professional. "I could search the area immediately before the culprit has a chance to hide the clues."

Miss Brewster sighed heavily and shook her head. "That won't be necessary. I'm sure it's all a big misunderstanding. The money has to be here, and we'll find it."

Wren leaned back with a disappointed sigh. If she was given a chance, she just knew she could solve the case in record time. Her dad had taught her a lot.

Miss Brewster rubbed her fingertips up and down the sides of her forehead. "Levi, please go to Mr. Gozzie's office and ask him to come here as soon as he has a free moment. Tell him it's urgent, but please let me explain the situation."

Levi nodded, jumped up and ran from the room.

Miss Brewster walked across the room. "While we're waiting on Levi, I will search the room. I want each of you to look in your own desk. There is a chance that someone is playing a joke on us and put the bag in a desk. If anyone finds the bag of money, bring it to me."

Just then Paula tossed a folded paper toward Wren. It landed on Wren's desk and started to fall off, but Wren caught it and looked at Paula.

"Read it," mouthed Paula.

Wren slowly unfolded the paper and read, "I want to hire you to find the money. I swear I didn't steal it. I'll pay you. Paula." Wren glanced up in surprise.

Paula lifted her brow questioningly. "Help me," she whispered.

Wren looked back down at the paper. It was very tempting to let Paula hire her, but it was even more tempting to let Paula be found guilty. She deserved every bad thing that could happen to her.

"Please," whispered Paula, her hands locked together on her desk.

Wren heard the whisper over the noise around her.

She read the note again. Should she let Paula hire her?

"I need your help," Paula whispered. Wren looked at Paula and finally shook her head. She wanted to solve the case, but she didn't want to have Paula Gantz for a client.

"Do you want me to beg?" hissed Paula, her eyes dark with anger and unshed tears.

Wren crumpled up the note and squeezed it into a tight ball in her fist. "Why should I help you, Paula Gantz?" Wren whispered.

Paula's face crumpled just like the note had. Giant tears filled her eyes. She turned away from Wren and sat very still.

Pity for Paula stabbed Wren's heart, but she forced it away. Paula was getting just what she deserved.

Wren slowly opened her fist and looked down at the note. With the very tips of her fingers she smoothed out the note, then looked over again at Paula.

4

THE CASE

Wren bit off a corner of her peanut butter and jelly sandwich just as Neil walked into the kitchen. They had both just returned home from school. Mom was still at her office. Dad was out talking to a client. And Philip was practicing football.

"Hi, Neil." Wren tried to sound chipper and happy. She didn't want to think about Paula and her troubles.

"Hi, Wren. I heard about the money being taken. I can't believe anything like that could happen at JCA." Neil's voice cracked and he beamed with pleasure.

"Mr. Gozzie said he didn't want the police involved yet. He has all the teachers looking for the money." Neil smeared a thick coat of crunchy peanut butter across a piece of wheat bread. "Nobody's found it yet, though."

Wren wrapped her hands around her glass of milk. "They should've let me search."

Neil grinned. "I thought you'd say that."

"Maybe I could have found it."

Neil inspected his bread with narrowed eyes before he looked at Wren again. "I think they think it was Paula."

Wren nodded. "I know, but I don't think she did it."

"You don't? I thought for sure you'd think so."

Wren shrugged. "Why should she take it? She doesn't need it."

"I hate to think anyone at JCA would steal."

"I know." Wren watched as Neil smeared grape jelly on top of the peanut butter. He smashed the top slice of bread in place, pushed it down hard and took a huge bite. His cheeks puffed out as he chewed the large bite.

Wren ran a finger down the side of her glass. "I tried to think of someone who would steal, and I couldn't think of anyone."

"I suppose you're going to do your detective work and solve the case."

Wren lifted her chin. "I'd like to try."

Neil sank to the chair across the table from her and bit into the side of his sandwich, leaving streaks of grape jelly on his cheeks.

With a shake of her head Wren looked away from him. If Bess saw Neil now with jelly on his face, she'd wonder how she could ever like him.

Neil drank half of his glass of milk, wiped his mouth, and said, "I feel kind of sorry for Paula."

Wren's eyes popped wide open. "What?"

"I do. She doesn't have anyone to tell her troubles to."

"Who cares?"

"God cares."

Wren flushed. "Besides God, I mean."

Neil nodded. "I might."

"She's so nosy, Neil!"

"Her parents are too busy to listen to her."

"She makes trouble for everyone!"

"I know."

"How can you feel sorry for her?"

Neil shrugged. "She's not a Christian, so she can't share her troubles with God and let Him help her."

Wren couldn't swallow her bite of sandwich. "I've been thinking about that lately."

"Her mom and dad want her to have everything. I think that's why they took her out of public school and put her in JCA."

Wren forced down her sandwich and glass of milk. She rinsed out her glass and set it on the counter beside the sink. "Paula asked me to help her."

Neil pushed away from the table. "Help her?"

"Find the thief. She wants to hire me." Wren waited for Neil to laugh, but he didn't.

"Are you going to take the case?"

Wren tucked her hair behind her ears. "I might." Startled by her own words, Wren's eyes popped wide open. Why had she said that? She'd turned Paula down flat.

"I think you should."

Wren sank back against the counter and stared at Neil. "I can't believe you said that."

Neil shrugged. "I'm learning to love my neighbor as myself. And Paula is definitely a neighbor."

Wren wrinkled her nose. "That's for sure."

"I've got work to do. See you later." He lifted his hand in a short wave and walked to his bedroom. The hum of the refrigerator sounded loud in the sudden silence.

Slowly Wren walked to the front room and looked across the street to Paula's house. As she watched, Wren saw Paula walk out her front door and sit down on the steps, her chin in her hands. She looked lonely and sad.

Wren sighed heavily. Paula deserved to be sad and lonely. It served her right to be suspected of stealing the money. She was always making trouble for everyone else. It was time trouble paid her a long visit.

Wren saw Paula rub her eyes and blow her nose, and Wren knew she was crying. Wren couldn't remember ever seeing Paula cry. It made her feel funny.

"Should I help her?" Wren turned away from the window, away from Paula's sad look.

In her heart Wren knew the answer, and she sighed loud and long. She knew Neil was right and that God did want her to love Paula.

"But that's impossible!" cried Wren, flinging out her arms.

A few minutes later Wren walked across the street and stopped at the bottom of the porch steps. "Hello, Paula."

Paula sniffed hard. "Hello."

"What's wrong?"

"What do you care?"

Wren walked up the three steps and sat beside Paula. A gust of wind blew dried leaves across the yard into the street. "I don't think you took the money, Paula."

"I didn't. But somebody wants to blame me. Who hates me that much?"

Wren could think of several people that might. "What did your parents say?"

"I couldn't tell them. Dad was upset about a suit brought against him, and Mom was trying to get him to hire a different lawyer. I didn't want to make them feel worse."

"Didn't you tell them anything about the missing money?"

"No."

"You should."

Paula shook her head. "I can't. Maybe the money will turn up tomorrow."

"Stolen money can't just turn up, Paula. Someone has to find it, or find the thief and make him return it. You can't ignore this, Paula. It won't go away."

Paula sniffed and said with a tiny catch in her voice, "I know."

"Why don't you go inside and tell your mom and dad."

"They left a while ago and won't be back until dinnertime."

Wren glanced at Paula. "Are you all alone?"

"Yes."

Wren had never seen Paula so defeated.

"I might help you." Wren wanted to grab the words back, but it was too late.

"You will?" Paula's face brightened.

"I said I might."

Paula's shoulders sagged. "Oh."

"Are you sure you don't know where the money is?"

"I'm positive! I put the bag in Miss Brewster's desk and it just disappeared!"

"It couldn't have just disappeared."

"I never saw anyone at the desk. Miss Brewster didn't notice anyone. I put the money in there just a few minutes before Miss Brewster called roll. And suddenly it was gone." Paula wrapped her arms across her chest and rocked back and forth. "And everyone thinks I did it. Nobody likes me. Nobody believes me."

Wren bit her lower lip and pressed her hands on her legs. Two girls rode by on bikes. Down the street a dog barked. Neil's words came back to her. I'm learning to love my neighbor as myself. She knew Jesus wanted her to do it too. She shook her head slightly. She couldn't love Paula after all the trouble she'd caused.

Wren moved uneasily. She knew God wanted her to obey His Word. She remembered the many, many times her dad had told her that she was never alone, that God was always with her to help her obey.

Silently she prayed for herself and for Paula.

"Why don't you go home if you're not going to help me?" said Paula, rubbing her nose with the back of her hand.

Wren took a deep breath. "I am going to help you, Paula."

Paula's eyes popped wide open. "You are?"

"I'll take your case."

"You will?"

"And I'll solve it."

Paula jumped up. "Don't just sit there. Get to work!"

Wren looked up at Paula and groaned. This wasn't going to be easy.

Slowly she pushed herself up. "Tell me every move you made this morning from the time you picked the bag of money up in the office until it was missing."

"But I already told you everything."

"Tell me again." Wren whipped out a tiny notebook and yellow stub of a pencil. "Start at the beginning and don't leave anything out. I want to get it all down."

5

BESS

The next day after school Wren went to Bess's house with her. Wren flipped open her new notebook to the page marked Bess. "I want to ask you a few questions, Bess."

Bess dropped her shoes in her closet. "About what?"

Wren's stomach tightened. "I took the case."

Bess studied Wren and was quiet a long time. "What case?"

"The case of the missing money."

Bess touched her forehead as if it ached. "Oh, dear."

Wren took a deep breath and let it out slowly. "I'm working for Paula."

"Paula Gantz?"

"Yes."

"I can't believe it!"

"And I want to ask you some questions."

Bess stepped back, bumped against her bed and dropped to the edge of it. Her blue eyes were wide with shock. "Do you suspect me of taking the money, Wren?"

"Everyone in the fifth-grade room is a suspect."

"But me? Me, Wren? Your very best friend?"

Wren nodded. She gripped her pencil between her fingers. She hated to upset her very best friend, but this was business. "Tell me where you were from the time you entered the school building until Miss Brewster discovered the money was missing."

Bess groaned. "I was with you, Wren."

"Every minute?"

"Yes! When I wasn't with you, I was sitting at my own desk. I didn't want any more trouble that would send us to the office." Bess jumped up, her hands trembling and her face suddenly pale. "Did Neil find out about us going to the office?"

Wren frowned. "Not from me."

"From anyone?"

"Not from anyone, Bess."

"Are you sure?"

"Not positive, but almost positive." Wren dropped to the chair beside Bess's desk. "He would've said something if he'd found out about it."

"You're sure?"

"Yes, Bess. You worry too much. Now, let's get down to business." Wren held her pencil over her notebook. "Did you notice anything suspicious yesterday morning in class?"

Bess paced back and forth across her bedroom. "Oh, Wren, how would I notice anything suspicious? I'm not a detective. I never want to be a detective."

Wren wrote DIDN'T NOTICE ANYTHING. Inside she groaned. How could Bess not notice anything?

Bess bent over Wren's shoulder to see the notebook. "Who else did you question?"

"You're the first. After I told Paula I'd take the case, I had to get a new notebook. I'm calling it The Case of the Missing Money. See?" Wren turned over the notebook to show Bess where she'd written the words with a bold black marker.

"I see all right," said Bess with a tired sigh.

"I have to keep an account of everything I learn about the case." Wren fingered the notebook lovingly. Someday she'd have an entire file full of notebooks.

"Do you think you'll fill that whole notebook?" asked Bess in surprise.

"I might. I write big." No matter how hard she tried to write small and neat like Dad, she couldn't manage it.

"Did you question Neil?" Bess's eyes lit up. "I want to listen when you do."

Wren sighed heavily. "Bess, Neil is in eighth grade, not fifth. I'm only going to question those in our class."

Bess looked disappointed. "Who will you talk to next?"

Wren flipped her notebook open to the first page and studied it carefully. "I called Tim and he's riding over.

He's still staying with Adam Landon, so it'll take him a little longer to get here."

"How is his mom?"

"He said that she's getting better. He said it's really hard for her not to drink, but she's getting help in the special hospital for alcoholics. Tim misses her."

"That's hard to believe. She always yelled at him and never took care of him."

"But he loves her and she's his mother." Wren couldn't imagine what it would be like to have an alcoholic mother. Her mom never drank and was always nice unless she was overtired or angry because of Wren's detective work.

Bess looked in her mirror, patted her hair and looked closely at her face. "What's Neil doing now?"

Wren rolled her eyes. Sometimes Bess made her tired. "Working on his computer."

Bess pressed her hands over her heart. "Could I go say hello?"

"No. You're going to help me."

"What?" Bess shook her head, then carefully pushed her blonde hair back in place. "I don't want to help solve this case. You know I can't get into trouble the way you do."

"I don't get into trouble!" Wren flushed and ducked her head. "Well, maybe sometimes. But I can't help it if I'm a detective and have the ability to notice everything."

"You mean you see a mystery even when there isn't one."

Wren shrugged. "This time there is a mystery, and I'm going to solve it."

"I want to see Neil. He might talk to me."

"You know he won't."

"He might."

"Bess, Neil is working on his computer. He won't talk to anyone when he's working on it, and you know it."

Bess sighed heavily. "I know." She walked to her dresser, rearranged her ceramic raccoon and her clown music box, then turned back to Wren. "All right, I'll help you. Tell me what you want me to do."

Wren flipped her notebook closed, pushed her pencil into her jeans' pocket and walked toward the door. "You can go with me to talk to Sean. He's on the list after Tim."

"Sean won't like being suspected."

"He'll understand. I think . . . I hope."

Bess led the way outdoors into the brisk October wind. She stopped on the back sidewalk. "He won't like it at all when he hears you're working for Paula Gantz."

Wren nodded. "I know. But he'll have to understand."

"Where's Paula now? She's usually hanging around, snooping on us." Bess looked across the yard as if she expected Paula to pop out from behind the bushes.

"I told her to try to tell her parents what happened yesterday. She said she would try, but she didn't think they'd want to hear about it."

"Maybe they'd write a check for the whole amount and then we could forget about the missing money."

Wren's heart jerked. "No! I'm going to solve this case, Bess!"

Bess was silent as they walked toward Wren's house. "I can't understand why you're helping Paula."

Wren stopped at their picnic table. Soon they'd have to put it away in the garage before the snow fell. "Neil told me that he is learning to love others the way God loves them."

Bess brightened. "Neil said that?"

Wren nodded. "I got to thinking about it, and I know Jesus wants me to love my neighbors as myself, too. Paula is my neighbor. With help from Jesus, I am going to love her. And that means helping her."

Bess made a face. "I guess that means I have to love her, too."

"Yep, you do." Wren smiled. "You know that anything is possible with God."

Bess smiled and nodded. "That's right, Wren!"

"And even if it sounds impossible, it is possible to love Paula." The words helped Wren even as she said them. She laughed and caught Bess's hand in hers. "We can love Paula. With God's help."

6

TIM'S NEWS

Wren walked with Bess to Sean's back door. The chilly fall wind blew against her back. "He's probably watching the triplets," said Wren.

Bess nodded. "They're so cute. It would be fun to have three five-year-old brothers."

"It might be," Wren said. But she sounded doubtful.

"Sometimes I think it's just terrible to be the only child."

Wren rolled her eyes. "Sometimes I think it's terrible to have Philip and Neil as brothers."

Bess gasped, her hand at her throat. "How can you say that? That's the worst thing you've ever said!"

"I can say it, all right. You don't know what it's like to listen to them and watch them and have to be teased by them all the time."

"I'd love it! And I thought you did too, Wren."

"I guess I do. It's just that it's not always easy to have brothers." Wren knocked on the back door and waited.

She could hear shouting and laughing from inside, then running.

The door burst open and a small blond boy said, "Hi. You can't come in."

"Who is it, Ronnie?" asked Sean from inside.

"Two girls," said Ronnie. "But they can't come in. They're strangers."

"We are not," said Bess.

"I'm Wren and this is Bess. We go to school with Sean." Wren smiled, but Ronnie just stared at her. Sean opened the door wider. His face turned red. "Hi. What did you want?"

"To talk to you," said Wren, gripping her notebook tighter. "May we come in?"

"Sure, come in," said Sean. He stepped aside for them to enter just as two copies of Ronnie ran into the room.

"I'm Bobby," said one.

"I'm Jimmy," said the other.

"Bet you can't tell us apart," said Bobby. The boys lined up in front of Wren, and she couldn't tell them apart. They all wore jeans and red pullover shirts, had blond hair cut short and wide blue eyes. It was fun to see them.

Wren laughed. "You're right, I can't tell you apart."

"I can't either," said Bess.

"I can," said Sean grimly. He looked hesitantly at Wren. "Why did you come?"

Before Wren could answer, Ronnie yelled at the top of his lungs and leapt on the other boys. They fell to the kitchen floor in a heap, shouting and laughing.

Sean's face turned brick red. "Sorry," he shouted. "We'll have to talk in the living room." He led the way. Wren and Bess followed him and sat on the couch.

Wren flipped open her notebook. "I want to ask you a few questions, Sean." She had to speak loudly over the noise of the triplets.

"Questions about what?" asked Sean, moving restlessly on his chair.

"The missing money," said Bess.

Sean jumped up. "I don't know anything about it! I said so in school. Did someone say I took it?"

"No, Sean. Please, sit down. This is just routine." Wren liked the sound of that so she said it again. "This is just routine. What I want to know is, what did you see yesterday morning that might help me find the person who took the money?"

"I didn't see anything. I think Paula took it. She's mean all the time, and it would be just like her to take it."

"She didn't take it," said Wren.

Sean scowled. "Since when did you become her friend?"

Suddenly the triplets burst into the room, yelling at the top of their lungs. Sean grabbed for the boys and shouted for them to be quiet. Wren knew that he always took care of them for an hour each afternoon to give his mother a break. Sean had told her that his mom took a walk or visited a friend, then came back refreshed and ready to handle her family again.

"Mom will be home soon, you guys," said Sean, "so be quiet!"

They dropped to the floor and looked like three angels sitting in a row. "Did you come to tell us a story?" one of the boys asked Wren.

"No." She glanced at Sean. "Can you answer my question now?"

"You didn't answer mine."

Wren moved restlessly and shot a look at Bess.

Bess rubbed her hands down her jeans. "The Bible says we're to love everyone and that includes Paula Gantz. Wren is helping Paula because God wants her to. She doesn't think Paula took the money."

"Oh," said Sean.

"So, will you answer my question?" asked Wren.

Sean took a deep breath. "I didn't see anything different at school yesterday morning. I was tired because the boys kept me awake the night before."

"We did," they said smugly.

Wren asked a few more questions but didn't get any answers. Finally she stood up and motioned to Bess. "We'd better get home. Tim might be there already."

"See you in school tomorrow, Sean," said Bess. "Bye, boys."

They leapt up and ran at her, all flinging themselves against her at the same time. "Bye," they shouted.

A few minutes later Wren stood outside the house and looked at Bess. Her hair was mussed and her jacket sleeve was smeared with jelly. "Do you still think it would be fun to have triplets in your family?"

Bess tried to smooth her hair back into place. "I think I'd rather visit them at Sean's house. I wouldn't want them every day all day long."

Wren laughed and led the way to their bikes. A few minutes later they rode up to her back door. Tim sat on the picnic table. He ran to them, smiling.

"Guess what?" he asked.

Wren studied him, feeling his excitement. His red hair stood up, and his freckles seemed to dance on his face. Her heart sank and she didn't want to guess, but finally she said, "You found the thief!"

"You did?" asked Bess happily. "That's great!"

Tim shook his head. "No, I didn't."

Wren's heart leapt and she laughed aloud. "Good. What's the news then?"

Tim pulled an envelope from his jacket pocket. "Adam wrote out a check to cover the entire amount that was stolen."

"What?" cried Wren in horror.

"I can't believe it," said Bess in awe, reaching out to touch the envelope. "That's a lot of money."

"Miss Brewster will be glad," said Tim. He looked very pleased with himself.

"Well, you can't give it to her!" cried Wren, grabbing the envelope and holding it to her chest.

"Hey, give that back!" cried Tim.

"Yes, do," cried Bess.

"I won't!" Wren shook her head. "You can't give it to Miss Brewster!"

Tim frowned. "What do you mean?"

"Yes, what?" asked Bess, looking worried.

"It's just not fair, Tim!" Tears pricked Wren's eyes.

"Wren!" cried Bess, plucking at Wren's sleeve. "Don't do this."

Wren stepped close to Tim with a pleading look in her dark eyes. "Tim, please understand. I have a case to solve. If we hand in this money, Miss Brewster won't let me solve my case."

"That's ridiculous, Wren," said Tim. "You could still find the missing money. Adam said it would take the pressure off Miss Brewster."

Wren shook her head hard enough to make her dark hair flip across her face. "But I need Miss Brewster to want me to find the money!"

He shook his head. "Adam wants to help our class. Give back that check so I can take it to Miss Brewster tomorrow!"

Wren stuffed the envelope into her pocket and

jumped away from Tim and Bess. "You can't have this money, Tim! Not until you promise to give it back to Adam Landon. I mean it!"

"Don't, Wren," said Bess.

"This is my case and I'm going to solve it! I want to solve it. I need to. Tim, you understand that, don't you?"

Tim walked toward Wren. "Give it back right now, Wren."

"No!"

"Give it back, Wren," whispered Bess with a shiver.

"You have to," said Tim grimly.

"I do not!" Wren backed away.

"Yes, you do, Wren," said Bess, wringing her hands helplessly.

Tim stopped just inches from Wren. "If you don't give it back, then that will be stealing, Wren House! Do you want to be just like the person who stole the money at school?"

"No," whispered Wren with a slight shake of her head.

"You will be just as bad if you keep that money." Tim pointed to her pocket. "Give it back now!"

"I . . . I can't, Tim. Don't make me!"

"It's not your money, and you can't keep it." Tim held out his hand. "Give it to me right now."

"I'll tell your dad if you don't," said Bess.

Tim turned on her, his face dark with anger. "No, you will not, Bess Talbot! You can't make trouble for Wren."

Wren looked at Tim in surprise.

Bess swallowed hard and backed away from Tim. "I won't tell her dad. I only said that to make her give back the money."

Tim turned to Wren and held out his hand without saying a word.

Wren slowly pulled out the envelope and held it out to Tim. Giant tears welled up in her dark eyes and slipped down her cheeks. Suddenly great sobs shook her and she couldn't stop crying.

Tim looked helplessly at her. "Don't, Wren. Please."

"Wren, stop crying," said Bess, shaking Wren's arm. "You're just doing it to make us feel sorry for you."

"I am not," said Wren with a hiccup between each word. "I don't want to give up my case."

Tim folded the envelope. "Wren, you can still solve the case even if I give this money to Miss Brewster."

"It just wouldn't be the same, Tim."

"Yes, it would," said Bess. "Don't talk him out of it, Wren."

Wren looked closely at Tim. Could she convince him to keep the money for a while? She saw the sympathy in Tim's eyes. "Tim, give me two days. Then you can hand in the check if I haven't found the missing money. Please. Oh, please, Tim!"

He shook his head.

"Don't do it, Tim," said Bess.

"Just give me two days to solve the case, Tim. If I haven't found the missing money or the person who took it, you can hand in this check and I won't say a word. I mean it. Honest." Wren waited, her heart in her throat.

Tim twisted his toe in the grass and watched a leaf blow across the yard. "Two days, Wren, but that's all. And I'll have to tell Adam about it."

"Oh, dear," said Bess weakly.

"Two days!" cried Wren. "I can do it, Tim. I know it!"

But could she? Wren pushed the terrible doubt to the back of her mind and flipped open her notebook to Tim's page.

7

QUESTIONS

Wren's fingers were cold, but she didn't want to go inside to be interrupted by her family. "Tim, tell me everything you saw yesterday morning when you got to school."

"Everything?"

"Pertaining to this case, of course."

"I'm cold, Wren," said Bess. "I want to go inside."

"In a minute, Bess. Listen to Tim and maybe something he says will help you remember an important incident."

Bess shrugged and wrinkled her nose. "I doubt it, but I'll stay."

Tim screwed up his freckled face in thought. "I walked into class behind David and Jim. They were talking about the newspaper subscriptions they'd sold. I sat at my desk and took out my math book. I had three problems to finish before I could hand in my paper."

Bess gasped.

"What?" asked Wren, suddenly alert.

"I forgot to hand in my math! Oh, dear, I'll get a zero for the day!"

"Forget it, Bess," snapped Wren. "We're talking real life here and you're thinking of division and multiplication." Wren turned back to Tim. "Keep going."

Tim scratched his head. "I finished my math and class started."

"Did you see Paula with the money bag?"

"No."

"You didn't?"

"No. I was busy."

Wren's shoulders sagged. She looked helplessly at the scribbled notes under Tim's name. None of it helped her case. "I thought for sure you'd be able to help me, Tim. You usually notice everything."

"If Paula took the bag, then no one would've noticed."

Paula jumped around a bush. "I didn't take the money! Don't say that I did!"

Bess shrieked and stumbled back. "You scared me!"

"You were spying!" cried Wren, shaking her finger at Paula.

Tim crossed his arms tightly against his chest.

"You know kids at school think you're guilty."

"Well, I'm not! Didn't you tell him, Wren?"

"I told him, but he doesn't believe me. And maybe I shouldn't believe you, either. You were spying on us."

"So what?" Paula tossed her head. "I have to know what's going on, don't I?"

"You could ask," said Bess, frowning.

Paula ignored Bess and stepped closer to Wren. "What have you learned since you got your notebook and started asking questions?" She reached for the notebook, but Wren held it close to her chest.

"No one reads this but me, Paula."

Paula pushed her hands into her jacket pockets hard. "What did you learn? Did you solve the case yet?"

"I'm good, but not that good," said Wren.

"I suppose you know about the check Adam Landon gave Tim," said Bess.

"Bess!" cried Wren, but it was too late.

"What check?" asked Paula. "Tim, what check?"

"Don't tell her," said Wren.

"Tell me!" cried Paula.

Tim shook his head. "You don't need to know."

Paula turned on Bess and grabbed her arms and shook her. "Tell me about the check, Bess! You tell me or I'll call Neil out here and tell him you like him. Everyone knows it but Neil, and if you don't tell me about the check, then even Neil will know."

Bess shook her head. Her cheeks were ashen and bright tears sparkled in her eyes. "Don't tell him. Please."

"I will."

"Leave her alone!" cried Wren.

"Get away from her," said Tim, tugging on Paula.

"Tell me, Bess," said Paula grimly. "Tell me right now."

Bess looked helplessly at Wren, then glanced at Tim.

"You'd better tell," said Paula sharply.

Bess shivered and glanced toward Wren's house. "Adam Landon wrote a check to cover the stolen money. Tim was going to give it to Miss Brewster tomorrow, but Wren won't let him. I said he should do it, but he said he'd wait for Wren."

Paula dropped her hands to her sides and glared at Tim. "You must think the money will never be found if you plan to hand in a check."

Tim shook his head. "I didn't say that. I just want to make sure our school can buy the copy machine in time for the program."

"That's Saturday afternoon," said Paula. "Wren, you will find the thief yet today, won't you?"

"I don't know, Paula. I'm going to try."

"But I hired you to find him or her! And now you don't think you can!"

"I can find the thief, but I don't know when. Tim said he would wait two days before he hands in the money. If I haven't solved the case by Friday afternoon, Tim will give the check to Miss Brewster."

"It's only fair," said Bess.

"I don't want fair," snapped Paula. "I want that money bag found, and I want the thief caught and punished! I don't want people blaming me for something I didn't do." She looked right at Tim and he shrugged.

"Stop fighting and let me do my work," said Wren. "I'm finished with Tim, and I'm going to question Joyce and Tina. They live near each other and only a block from here."

"I don't want to go with you," said Bess. "Don't make me, Wren."

"I wouldn't make you, Bess. Go home if you want."

Bess looked hopefully at Wren's house in case Neil was in sight, then turned and ran to her house.

"I'm going with you," said Paula firmly.

"No." Wren shook her head. "With you there, the girls would be afraid to answer my questions. They wouldn't want you mad at them."

Paula's brows shot up to her bangs. "Do they think I'm guilty?"

"A lot of people do," said Tim.

Paula threw up her hands. "I am not guilty! I'm not!" She pushed her nose right up to Wren's. "Get to work and prove I'm not. I'll go home, but you call me when you learn anything."

"I will." Wren sighed heavily as she watched Paula run across the street to her house. "Tim, this won't be easy."

"You're right." Tim picked up his ten-speed. "Let's go see Joyce and Tina."

Wren smiled. "I didn't think you'd want to help me."

"We're both detectives, aren't we?" Tim grinned, and Wren laughed aloud.

A few minutes later they stopped outside Tina's house where they found both Tina and Joyce on the porch.

"Hi, girls," said Wren.

They glanced up in surprise. "Hi, Wren," said Joyce.

"Hi, Tim," said Tina. "Are you two trying to sell more subscriptions?"

Wren sat on the edge of a bench that held plants on either end. She flipped open her notebook. "I want to ask a few questions."

"Are you trying to solve the mystery of the disappearing money?" asked Joyce with a laugh.

"I bet you are," said Tina, giggling.

Wren flushed painfully.

"We're both working on it," said Tim. He sat beside Wren. "What's your first question, Wren?"

"Are you going to write down our answers?" asked Tina.

"This makes me nervous," said Joyce.

Wren poised her pencil over her notebook. "I write down everything so that I can go over it later to make sure I didn't miss anything. All great detectives do that." She glanced from one girl to the other. Hopefully they'd stop laughing at her and take her seriously. "Joyce, tell me if you saw the money bag yesterday morning."

Joyce shrugged. "I saw it when Paula was zipping it closed."

Wren's heart lurched. "Zipping it closed?"

Joyce nodded. "Paula zipped it, and that's all I saw."

"Didn't you see her give the bag to Miss Brewster?" asked Tim.

"No, I turned to talk to Tina."

"About the program," said Tina.

Wren scribbled in her notebook. "Did you see the money bag, Tina?"

"No. But I already told Miss Brewster that."

"Did either one of you see anything suspicious?" asked Wren, feeling desperate.

"Nothing," they said, shaking their heads.

Wren drew a sad face on the corner of the page. "Did anyone approach Paula while the money was in her hands?"

"I wasn't watching," said Tina.

"I didn't notice," said Joyce.

Slowly Wren closed her notebook and stood up. Disappointment rose inside her, and she tried to push it away. "If you think of anything, let me know." She said good-bye and walked to the bikes with Tim. Back in her yard she let her breath out in a loud sigh.

"Maybe you should give up," said Tim.

"What? Never!"

"I knew you'd say that." Tim pulled the envelope from his pocket. "It's not too late to change your mind about this."

"I will solve this case, Tim!" Her voice rang across the yard. "I won't give up."

Paula jumped from behind the bushes. "It's a good thing, Wren House."

Wren groaned. "Are you spying again?"

"I saw you ride up, and I wanted to know what Joyce and Tina said."

"They didn't see anything important," said Tim.

"Is it hopeless, Wren?" asked Paula with a catch in her voice.

Wren thought about it for a while, then shook her head. "It's not hopeless. We'll pray that God will show us where the money is."

"Will He do that?" asked Paula in surprise.

"God answers prayer," said Tim. "I know." He nodded his head, a faraway look in his eyes.

"God does answer because He said He would in the Bible," said Wren. She knew she sounded like their pastor, but she also knew that it was true. "He'll help us find the money and the person who took it."

Paula looked down at the grass, then up at Wren. "I don't know how to pray."

Wren quickly hid her surprise. "Prayer is talking to God."

"Will you pray?" asked Paula just above a whisper.

Wren glanced at Tim and he smiled and nodded. She bowed her head and said, "Heavenly Father, thank You for the wisdom that You've given us. Thank You that You love us and gave us Jesus to be our personal Savior. In Jesus' name help us to find the money and the person that took it. Help us to love each other and help each other. And when we find the thief, help us to forgive him. Thank You. In Jesus' name. Amen."

"Amen," said Tim.

"Amen," whispered Paula. She flicked a tear off her cheek, then turned and ran home.

Wren frowned thoughtfully. "I don't think Paula has ever asked Jesus to be her Savior."

"I don't think so either."

Wren turned to Tim. "I think this case may be a good thing. Maybe I'll get to talk to her about it."

8

DAD'S ADVICE

Tim and Wren watched Paula open her front door and slip inside. A black car drove past, sending fallen leaves swirling. "I'll wait and talk to Paula tomorrow. I have to get inside and help with dinner. Want to eat with us, Tim?"

"No. I have to get to Adam's—I mean Dad's." Tim's voice was full of pride. "We always have dinner at his house."

Wren knew it had been different at his mother's home. Most of the time he'd eaten a bowl of cornflakes for his meals. Wren was glad Adam and his family were taking good care of Tim. She knew Tim was glad too. "See you at school in the morning, Tim."

He nodded. "I won't forget to pray for Paula, and for you to find the money and the thief."

"Thanks, Tim." Wren smiled and watched him ride away, then turned to go into the house.

"Wren! Wait!"

Wren glanced back to see Bess running toward her. Bess looked as if she'd been crying. Her jacket was unzipped and flapping, and her tennis shoes were untied. "What's wrong, Bess?"

Bess stopped just inches from Wren. "I had to talk to you."

"Oh?"

"But I didn't want Tim to hear."

"He's gone."

"I know." Bess bit her bottom lip and blinked back tears. "Are you mad at me?"

"Mad at you? Why?"

Bess locked her fingers together in front of her. "For telling Paula about the check from Adam Landon."

Wren shook her head. "No. No, I'm not mad. I didn't want you to tell, but I'm not mad."

Bess sighed in relief. "I'm glad. I know I should've been strong and brave and not let her force me to tell, but I just couldn't not tell."

Wren smiled reassuringly. "It doesn't matter."

"I didn't want her to tell Neil that I like him."

"I know, Bess."

"But I shouldn't have told her."

"She didn't want the check handed in, either."

Bess gripped Wren's arm. "Won't you please let Tim give it to Miss Brewster? It would be so much better for the school—for everyone."

Wren stubbornly shook her head. "He gave me two days and I'm taking them. I'm sure I'll know the answers by then."

"I hope so."

"Me, too," said Wren, thinking of all the questions she still had to ask.

Bess shivered. "I guess I'd better go home." She glanced toward Wren's house. "I would like to see Neil once more today."

Wren shifted her notebook from one hand to the other. "Bess, I don't know about you sometimes. But come in and see him if you want to that badly."

Bess hung back, suddenly frightened. "What if he knows I went in just to see him?"

"Neil?" Wren chuckled. "He wouldn't think of that. Come on."

Bess hesitated. "Should I really?"

"Yes! Come on, before you get too scared and run home." Wren tugged on Bess's arm. "One look and you can go home again."

"Maybe he'll talk to me," Bess said softly.

"Maybe." Wren doubted it, but she knew Bess was always hopeful.

Wren led Bess inside and followed voices to the kitchen where everyone was working on dinner.

"It's about time you came in, Wren," said Philip. "Hi, Bess. Are you eating with us?"

"No." Bess glanced at Neil, but he was busy peeling a carrot.

"You're welcome to stay," said Lorrene House, smiling over her shoulder from where she stood in front of the oven. "We're having meat loaf, and it's almost done."

"And a salad," said Sam House with a grin as he held up a head of lettuce. "Neil and I are tossing it together." Sam laughed and nudged Neil. "Right, Neil?"

"Right, Dad." Neil grinned at his dad and looked back at his peeler.

"I have to get home," said Bess. "Bye. Bye, everyone." She waited and finally Neil looked at her, smiled, and said good-bye with the others. Wren saw the look of joy on Bess's face before she walked out of the kitchen ahead of Wren.

"See you in the morning, Bess," said Wren.

Bess nodded and closed the back door with a gentle click.

Back in the kitchen Wren hid a smile as she washed her hands and dried them on a yellow hand towel. Today was her day for setting the table and helping with dishes after the meal.

Smells of potatoes, broccoli, and meat loaf made her stomach growl with hunger. As Philip talked about his part-time job, Wren picked up a chunk of the mild cheddar cheese that Dad had cut into the salad bowl and bit into it. It tasted better than she'd expected and she picked out another piece.

"That's all, Wren," said Sam, grinning. "Save it for dinner."

"I'm hungry."

"Dinner will be ready in a minute," said Lorrene.

"Set the table fast, Wren," said Philip. "This is one night you're not getting out of it."

Wren frowned. "Did I say I didn't want to set the table?" She glanced at her notebook on the counter beside the refrigerator. "I plan to work on my case after dinner."

"Your case?" asked Neil with a smile.

"I decided to help Paula."

"Good for you," said Neil.

"What's this all about?" asked Sam.

"Will it take you a long time to answer that question?" asked Lorrene.

"Maybe," said Wren.

"Then please save it until we're at the table. Then we can all listen while we eat." Lorrene sliced the meat loaf and set in on the table near the steak sauce and catsup.

Wren carried the flowered china plates to the table and put them in place with the silverware beside them. She filled glasses with water, dropped ice cubes into them, and set them above the knives.

After Philip asked the blessing on the food, Sam said, "Now, Wren, tell us about your case."

Wren shot a look at her mom. Mom sometimes got nervous when Wren talked about detective work. But since she'd solved a few mysteries already, Mom was beginning to relax a little about it.

"I told them about the missing money," said Neil, reaching for the broccoli.

"I know how bad Miss Brewster must be feeling," said Lorrene.

"It's a terrible shame that it happened," said Sam, pouring dressing over his salad.

"Everyone was upset," said Wren. "Especially Paula."

"Poor Paula." Lorrene took a bite of meat loaf.

"Poor Paula?" asked Philip with a laugh. "That little girl deserves everything she gets."

"She needs help," said Sam.

"I guess you're right, Dad," said Philip as he spooned creamy mashed potatoes onto his plate.

Wren nodded. "She hired me to solve the case."

"That's a new one," said Philip. He turned to Lorrene. "Mom, I lost the button off my blue shirt. Do you know where I can find one for it?"

Lorrene dabbed the corners of her mouth with her napkin. "You'll have to look in the chest beside the sewing machine."

"Did you really accept her as a client, Wren?" asked Sam, his eyebrow cocked.

Wren nodded again.

"That's putting God's love into action," said her dad, making Wren feel wonderful.

"I already looked there, Mom," said Philip. "Any other suggestions?"

"What have you accomplished so far, Wren?" asked Neil, stabbing his fork into his meat loaf.

"I questioned a few of the fifth graders." Wren scooted to the edge of her chair. "I have a notebook, and I wrote down what each one said. None of them saw anything important."

"You can never tell," said Sam.

Lorrene chewed her salad with a thoughtful look on her face, then finally said, "I think you could find a button in that little dish above the washer, Philip."

"That's right!" Philip nodded with a pleased smile. "I saw a few buttons there yesterday when I did the laundry."

Wren sighed heavily. "Sometimes I wonder if I'm writing down anything important."

Sam nodded as he laid his fork on his plate and leaned forward. "Wren, even a tiny observation can be a big clue. Never overlook anything. Act as if everything you hear and write down is valuable information for your case."

"But how can I sort through everything?"

"You study what you have, you think of what you saw yourself, and you put it together."

Wren sighed heavily. "I don't think I saw anything."

"I saw a blue button on the bathroom floor," said Neil.

Wren frowned at him before she turned back to listen to Dad.

"But you might have. Each student might've seen something, and once you piece it all together, just like a puzzle, you'll see the whole picture."

Wren smiled. "That makes sense. Thanks, Dad."

Sam winked at her and she felt warm all over. "You're very welcome."

"Tomorrow I'll talk to more kids. Somebody might have something important to say." Wren bent over her plate and ate while her head spun with thoughts about the case of the missing money.

9

MORE QUESTIONS

Wren watched the rain lash against the car as her dad drove toward Jordan Christian Academy. She glanced at Bess to ask her something, but bit back the question. Bess was so engrossed in Neil beside her that she'd never hear anything.

"I think I should have a car of my own," said Philip from the front passenger seat. "That way I could drive us to school on days like this and save you the bother, Dad."

Sam grinned knowingly. "It's no bother, Philip."

"I'm going to start saving for a car," said Neil.

Bess smiled as if he'd said golden words to her alone.

"It's never too early to start saving," said Sam.

Wren had heard this discussion hundreds of times.

"I have almost two hundred dollars saved for a car," said Philip.

"Good for you. Keep it up and soon you'll be able to buy one." Sam stopped outside JCA. "I'll pick you up after school if it's still raining."

"I saw a car advertised on the bulletin board at school for only $800. Can we look at it, Dad?"

Wren sighed. Philip never got tired of looking at cars, even the ones he knew Dad wouldn't let him buy. "Thanks for the ride, Dad." Wren leaned up and kissed her dad's cheek. "Have fun on your case."

"You, too, Wren. Bye, Bess. Neil. Philip, get the address and we'll take a look tomorrow."

"Thanks, Dad. I already have the address. We could go now. It wouldn't matter if I missed my first hour."

Rain whipped against the car. Sam shook his head. "Never look at a car in the rain, son. See you later." He slipped a big hand around Philip's neck, pulled him close, and hugged him hard.

"Bye, Dad," said Philip, smiling.

"Want to look with us, Neil?" asked Sam, glancing back at Neil.

Neil grinned and nodded. "Maybe I can buy it." His voice cracked. He squared his shoulders and looked around to make sure everyone had noticed.

"No way," said Sam with a wink at Neil.

Wren hesitated another second, then flung open the door and raced for the school, her precious notebook inside her school bag. Philip and Neil sped around to hit the school door first and Bess followed, holding her yellow umbrella just right so the rain wouldn't touch her hair.

Wren held the door open from inside the building. "Hurry up, Bess."

Bess stepped inside, shook her umbrella carefully and stood it in the corner of the hallway to dry beside two others. Slowly she turned. "Where's Neil?" she whispered.

Wren shrugged. "Probably in his room by now."

Bess let out her breath in relief. "Good. I look awful and I didn't want him to see me."

Wren hung up her jacket in the coatroom before she turned back to Bess. "You look fine."

"But look!" Bess pointed to three wet spots on her skirt. "I'm a mess! How can I get dried off?"

Wren rolled her eyes. "Go in the rest room, turn on the hand dryer and point it at your skirt. I'm going to talk to a few more people."

Bess dashed away and Wren looked down the hall toward the fifth-grade room. Jim, Jason, and Kris stood there. Wren flipped open her notebook and frowned. She didn't have a page for Kris. How could she have forgetten her? Quickly Wren wrote KRIS, then strode down the noisy hall to speak to her. Only Jim and Jason stood there.

"Hi," said Wren. "Where did Kris go?"

"I didn't notice," said Jim.

"Probably inside," said Jason.

Wren turned to Jim's page. How could they not have noticed where Kris had gone?

With her pencil ready, Wren looked at Jim. "I'd like to

ask you a few questions about Tuesday, Jim." Jason started to walk away and she held out her hand. "You, too, Jason."

"I heard you were trying to find the thief," said Jim.

"Don't start thinking I took the money," said Jason sharply.

"I just want to ask you if you saw Paula with the bag of money Tuesday morning."

"I did," said Jim.

Wren's heart leapt. "And?"

Jim spread his hands and shrugged. "She was walking from the office to our room."

"Then what?"

Jim dropped his hands to his sides. "I went to the rest room and didn't see what she did."

"Oh." Wren scribbled the information down. "What about you, Jason?"

"I got to school late that day, so I didn't know anything until Miss Brewster said she couldn't find the bag."

Wren studied Jason for a few seconds. It was very embarrassing to learn that she didn't notice everything around her at all times. "I didn't realize you were late."

"I walked in quietly and gave Miss Brewster a note from my mom at recess."

"Was anyone else late that you know of?" asked Wren.

"Kris was. I saw her when my mom dropped me off."

Wren made a note to ask Kris about being tardy. "Jason, did you see anything that made you suspicious when you walked into the classroom?"

"Suspicious, Wren? You're the only one who sees suspicious things." Jason laughed and nudged Jim.

Wren flushed. "I am a detective, you know."

"Oh, sure," said Jim, chuckling. He pushed Jason to the doorway and inside.

Wren ignored the remark and glanced around for Kris, spotted Russ, and waited for him. "Hi, Russ."

His face turned brick red and he looked down at his feet. "Hi," he mumbled.

"Russ, did you see Paula with the money bag Tuesday morning?"

"No."

"Did you say no?"

"Yes."

"Russ, it's hard to hear you." Wren poised her pencil over her notebook. "Did you see the money bag at all Tuesday morning?"

"No." He wouldn't look up, and his voice was lost against his thin chest.

"Did you see anything suspicious?"

"No."

Impatiently Wren flipped back her hair. "Who did you see when you walked into class Tuesday?"

"Nobody."

Wren wanted to shout for him to hold up his head and speak so she could hear more easily. "Did you hear Miss

Brewster say the money bag was missing?"

"Yes."

"Where did you look for it?"

"My desk. The back bookcase."

"Did you find anything?"

"My pencil."

Wren gave up. "Thanks anyway, Russ."

He walked away, his head down, his face red. She knew why he hadn't seen anything.

With a sigh she looked around. She had to question David and Kris and then she'd be finished with everyone in fifth grade. "Finished until I think of more questions," she muttered.

Inside the room she looked around for David or Kris, and found David looking at the aquarium. She walked to his side. "Hi, David."

"Hi, Wren. Look. The algae fish has grown more."

Wren glanced at it quickly, then turned her attention to her notebook. "David, I'd like to know if you saw Paula with the money bag on Tuesday morning."

David screwed up his face as if in deep thought. "I can't remember."

"What do you remember?"

"I fed the fish and checked to see that the air filter was working right. It wasn't, so I fixed it."

Wren bit back an impatient remark. "Did you see anything unusual?"

"One of the fish was playing hide-and-seek with another one."

"I mean about the money bag."

David tapped his finger against his lips. "I saw Brian Davies taking pictures."

"Brian Davies?" Her heart skipped a beat.

"He takes pictures for the newspaper and he was standing in the hallway taking pictures. I ducked so he couldn't get me." David laughed and looked proud of himself.

Wren slowly wrote BRIAN DAVIES. She started to draw a heart around his name, then stopped herself. She was a professional. Professional investigators didn't draw hearts around names even if they liked that person. She quickly made the note that Brian had been taking pictures. Now she'd have a reason for talking to him. Her mouth went dry and butterflies fluttered in her stomach.

"I think someone's been overfeeding the fish," said David, peering closely at the bright fish.

"Did you see anyone else?"

"I saw lots of kids. Do you want me to name them all?"

"I guess so."

"All the first and second graders?"

"Never mind." Wren flipped her notebook closed. "Did you see Kris?"

"She lives near me."

"I didn't know that."

David grinned. "I didn't think you did. That's why I told you."

Wren took a deep breath. "Did you see her this morning?"

"I think she's sick again today."

"I saw her a few minutes ago in the hallway."

David shrugged. "I thought she was still sick."

"I guess not." Wren looked around for Kris, but she wasn't in the room yet.

The bell rang and Wren watched everyone rush to their desks.

"Better sit down," said David.

"I will." She stayed beside the aquarium for a moment, though, and surveyed the room. One desk besides hers was still empty.

Thoughtfully she walked to her desk and sat down.

10

THE NOTE

Wren listened to Miss Brewster take roll. The classroom was silent except for the reply of "here" when Miss Brewster called each name and the splash of rain against the windows.

"Kris Bower," said Miss Brewster.

There was no answer and Wren looked over and back at the empty desk. Had Kris left school or was she in the hall or rest room?

David's hand shot up. "Miss Brewster."

"Yes, David."

"I think she's sick."

Wren frowned.

Miss Brewster raised a well-shaped eyebrow. "Oh?"

"She was sick yesterday and the day before." David looked around as if he was proud that he knew something that the others didn't know.

Miss Brewster looked down at her book. "Yes, yes, she was absent those days."

Wren flipped to the page marked KRIS in her notebook and wrote, ABSENT TUESDAY, WEDNESDAY, AND THURSDAY. While Miss Brewster finished taking roll, Wren glanced toward the door with a frown. She'd seen Kris in the hallway before class started. But now she was absent. Wren snapped her book closed. She had no reason to question Kris. She'd missed three days of school. She couldn't have any answers for the case.

Absently she flipped through her notebook. Brian Davies's name popped off the page and into her heart. She smiled. At the noon break she'd find a way to ask him about taking pictures. Maybe he'd clicked his camera at the right time to give her a clue. Dad had often told her that one picture was worth a thousand words.

"Wren?"

Wren's head shot up. "Yes?"

Miss Brewster smiled and shook her head. "Are you with us?"

The students snickered and Wren flushed. "What do you mean?"

"I've asked you three times if you'd ask your dad to call me."

Wren swallowed hard. "I'm sorry. I didn't hear you."

"I noticed. Will you ask your dad to call me?"

Wren's stomach tightened. "Do you need him professionally?"

Miss Brewster nodded. "I've decided to ask him to

help us find the missing money."

Wren's heart zoomed to her feet. She wanted to solve the case, not have Dad do it. She couldn't speak around the tight lump in her throat.

Tim waved his arm back and forth frantically.

"Yes, Tim," said Miss Brewster.

"I think Mr. House is too busy to take another case right now."

Wren shot Tim a thankful look, and he nodded slightly to let her know he'd seen her look and understood it.

Miss Brewster walked around her desk and leaned back against it. "I talked to Sam House just before I walked into class, and he said that he would do what he could as soon as possible."

Tears pricked Wren's eyes and she kept her head down so nobody would notice. Dad knew she was working on the case. How could he take it right from under her nose?

"Wren?"

Wren swallowed hard and said in a tiny voice, "Yes?"

"Would you please ask your dad to call me?" Miss Brewster peered down at Wren and waited for an answer.

"I'll tell him," Wren whispered. She wanted to look at Tim for sympathy, but she knew if she did, he would look sorry for her and she'd burst into tears.

Miss Brewster walked around her desk. "Class, open

your science books, please."

A note plopped on Wren's desk and she grabbed it before it fell to the floor. Slowly she unfolded it and read, "But I hired you to find the money and the thief." It was signed Paula.

"Passing notes, Wren?" asked Miss Brewster.

Wren froze and looked up at Miss Brewster with startled eyes.

"Bring it to me, please." Miss Brewster held out her hand. She looked very stern and Wren trembled.

Before Wren could move, Paula grabbed the note. "I'll read it to you, Miss Brewster."

"Thank you, Paula, but I'll read it for myself." Miss Brewster strode across the room and held out her hand.

Paula looked up into the teacher's eyes, and finally dropped the note into her outstretched palm.

While Miss Brewster read the note, Paula hung her head and sank back in her desk. No one else made a sound and Wren held her breath.

Finally Miss Brewster sighed, "Paula, Paula. When will you learn?"

Wren saw Paula blink hard as if blinking back tears.

"You will write twenty-five times, 'I will not write notes in class,' and hand it in before you go home today."

Paula swallowed hard before she said quietly, "Yes, Miss Brewster."

Wren waited, looking anxiously at Miss Brewster, but

she shook her head again, smiled slightly and walked back to her desk saying, "Open your science books, class."

Later, at recess, Wren walked outdoors with Bess. Wren could feel that Bess was ready to burst with questions. "Wait until we're outside," whispered Wren.

"I can't wait," hissed Bess.

"You'd better wait," snapped Paula.

Wren glanced over her shoulder to find Paula on their heels. "You caused trouble again, Paula. Won't you ever stop?"

Paula zipped up her jacket and opened the door for Wren and Bess. Cool wind blew against them. Puddles stood here and there. Paula stopped the girls near the swings. "I didn't mean to make trouble."

Curious, Bess asked, "What was in the note?"

"I told Wren that she had promised to take my case. I don't want it to go to her dad. He doesn't like me. Nobody does. And he'll blame me. I just know it."

"He will not!" cried Wren. "My dad is honest!"

"I didn't say he wasn't," said Paula.

"Yes, you did." Wren doubled her fists. "He wouldn't blame you unless you were guilty."

"He is honest," said Bess, nodding. She studied Paula closely. "Guilty of what?"

Paula rolled her eyes. "Where've you been, Bess? Guilty of taking the money, of course."

"Oh, that. But Wren's going to solve that case."

Wren nodded. "Yes, I am. And Dad knows it. I'm sure he won't really take the case away from me." Wren moved restlessly. Sometimes adults did things that she didn't understand. Dad might take the case just because he thought Miss Brewster and the school needed an adult detective.

From behind her Tim said, "You'll have to solve the case before he has a chance to, Wren."

She whirled around with a glad cry. "You're right, Tim!"

"Get it done," said Paula. "Don't you have questions to ask and answer—or something?"

"Yes! Yes, I do!" Wren gripped her notebook tightly. She'd felt so badly that she'd almost left it in her desk. She was glad she hadn't.

"I know you can solve the case, Wren," said Tim.

"You'd better solve it," said Paula grimly.

"I think you should let your dad," said Bess. When the others glared at her, she blinked and said, "Well . . ."

Wren flipped open her notebook. "I think I'll start by reading over everything that I wrote down."

She walked to a swing, sat down, and with her arms around the chains, opened her notebook, and began to read.

11

BRIAN'S PICTURES

After lunch Wren hurried from the cafeteria to look for Brian Davies. Her stomach fluttered and a shiver ran down her spine. It had been hard to eat lunch with Bess and Tim as if nothing was going to happen to her moments after. She had forced herself to talk as if everything was normal.

"My red-letter day," whispered Wren, beaming. Mom called days red-letter days when something extra special was going to happen.

She stopped near the back door that led to the playground. Her mouth was bone dry and her hand trembled as she pushed open the door.

She saw him almost immediately. How handsome he looked dressed in dark pants and a plaid shirt under a tan jacket that zipped up the front. He pushed his glasses in place as he listened to three eighth-grade boys around him. One of them was Neil. Wren gripped her notebook tighter. Should she pretend that she wanted to speak to

Neil and then talk to Brian?

Before she could move, Neil called, "Wren! Come here!"

For a moment she couldn't move, then she ran to him and said, "Hi." She looked right at Brian and said breathlessly, "Hi, Brian." Then to keep from looking so obvious she spoke to the other two boys. "Pete. Gene."

"We heard about Miss Brewster asking Dad to solve the case," said Neil.

Wren's heart sank and she nodded.

"Maybe now something will be done," said Gene.

"The thief should be kicked out of JCA," said Pete.

"Just so Mr. House finds the money and gets it back," said Brian.

Wren started to speak up, but Neil gave her a warning look. She closed her mouth and rubbed a hand across her notebook. She knew Neil didn't want to listen to the teasing she'd get if she said she was going to solve the case.

The boys talked a few more minutes about Miss Brewster, Sam House, and the case. Wren stood quietly by, happy to be close to Brian. Finally Neil said, "Let's get the soccer ball and play a while."

The boys started away, and Wren took a deep breath. "Brian, could I talk to you a minute?"

He shrugged and stopped while the others ran on. "Sure." He stood with his hands in his jacket pockets and his feet apart.

Her hands shook as she flipped open her notebook. She flushed as she thought about the heart that she'd almost drawn around Brian's name. If he'd seen a red heart around his name, he'd never have talked to her again. "David said you took pictures. I thought maybe you snapped a picture that would help us know who stole the money bag."

"I doubt it, or I'd have noticed." His voice cracked and he looked as proud as Neil.

She smiled to let him know she'd noticed. "Could you show me the pictures?"

"I guess."

"Now?"

He glanced toward the other boys across the school yard. "I guess so."

Shivers of delight ran over Wren and she smiled. "Thanks."

"They're in my desk." He strode toward the door and she ran to keep up with him.

She glanced around to see if Bess was watching. This was something she wanted Bess to see. Later they could talk about it in great detail. Wren bit back a giggle.

Inside the eighth-grade room Brian opened his desk and pulled out a folder. He opened it and snapshots fanned out. "Here they are."

"Thanks, Brian." His name slipped off her tongue like honey. She wanted to say it again, but she didn't. She picked up the photos and forced herself to concentrate on them. She was a professional, and she couldn't let anyone, not even Brian Davies, make her forget that.

She glanced over the pictures, but didn't see anything suspicious. She saw one of Kris Bower looking over her shoulder as she walked out the front door. She held it up to Brian. "When did you take this?"

He took it and studied it. "Tuesday or today."

"Probably today. She wasn't here Tuesday."

Wren took the picture back and looked at it again. Something nagged at her, but she couldn't pinpoint anything. Dad had said that when something nagged at her, she should let it set in the back of her mind and not force herself to remember. He said thinking about it made it push farther and farther away. If she just let it go, it'd pop into her mind when she least expected it. Finally she dropped the picture on the pile. "Thanks, Brian. Do you have any others to show me that you took Tuesday?"

"No." He closed the folder and stuck it back in his desk. "Wait. I did send some to the high school students to copy for the paper."

"I'd like to see them."

Brian shrugged and pushed his glasses against his face. "I'll get them back later today. I could show you after school if you want."

His words were pure gold to her. "I'd like that," she said in a careful voice. Could he see the sparkle in her eyes or hear the thud of her heart?

"See you later then," he said with a smile that lit up his dark eyes.

Wren walked on a cloud to where Bess sat on the swings. "Did you see, Bess?"

Bess stopped her swing and giggled. "I saw. You walked into school together. Tell me everything."

Wren looked around to make sure no one was close enough to overhear her. "Neil wanted to talk to me and he was walking with Brian, so I said 'hi' to Brian. He said 'hi' back." Wren sank onto a swing and rested her head against the chain. "He talked to me. He actually talked to me, Bess! I thought I'd burst. But I acted normal and didn't squeal or faint or anything."

"Tell me every word that Brian said."

Wren repeated the entire conversation and Bess listened, her eyes dreamy. "I'm meeting Brian right after school."

"You're so lucky, Wren."

Wren smiled. "I know."

The rest of the day dragged for Wren and finally, when the bell rang, she rushed into the hallway to catch Brian before he left the building. She didn't want him to forget that he'd agreed to meet her.

"What's the hurry, Wren?" asked Tim.

"I have to talk to someone." She peered around the noisy crowd in the hallway, anxious to go.

Tim nudged her arm. "Did you learn anything new?"

"Not yet."

"I could walk home with you and help you do some deductive reasoning."

Any other time Wren would have been glad for Tim's help. "Don't you have to hurry home?"

Tim's face lit up. "No. Adam said I could go to your place for a while."

Wren frantically searched for an answer and finally found it. "I have something to do right now. You walk with Bess and I'll meet you at my house in a while."

Tim shrugged and the sparkle left his eyes. "All right."

Wren watched him walk away to find Bess, but before she could move, Paula ran to her.

"Did you learn anything today?" asked Paula breathlessly.

"No." Wren looked helplessly down the hall.

"You don't have much time, you know."

"I know."

Paula shook Wren's arm. "You'd better hurry up and solve this before your dad does."

Wren nodded and pulled free. "I'm trying to."

"I'm going to walk home with you so you can tell me everything you know." Paula looked very stubborn and Wren knew she meant it.

"I have a clue to track down first," said Wren desperately. "I'll see you at home."

Paula frowned. "Are you trying to get rid of me?"

"I work better alone, Paula."

Paula sighed heavily. "I'm staying with you."

"You can't! I mean it. I do work better alone."

"Oh, all right! But I want to talk to you when you get home." Paula marched away in a huff.

Wren dashed to the eighth-grade room only to find that Brian had already gone. Her heart sank. She leaned against the wall and sighed.

"What's wrong, Wren?" asked the eighth-grade teacher.

Wren shot up. "Nothing."

"Are you sure?"

Wren licked her lips. "I was supposed to meet someone. Brian Davies."

"He left a little early for some reason. His mother came for him."

"That's strange." Wren smiled weakly, said good-bye, and walked slowly out of the school. A cool wind blew her skirt against her legs. She tucked her notebook under her arm and zipped her jacket. Why had Brian gone home early? Was something wrong at their house?

Wren ran down the empty sidewalk and crossed the street. A dog barked from behind a wire fence. No students were in sight. A horn honked. An eddy of leaves danced down the middle of the street. Wren stopped outside Brian's house. Dare she ring the doorbell and ask to see Brian?

"It's for the case," she said, squaring her shoulders. With her chin high she marched to the front door and rang the bell. No one answered and she rang again. She waited, but finally turned and walked slowly home.

"Wren!" Tim ran to her as soon as she entered the yard. She could see Bess waiting near the picnic table.

"Hi. I didn't get anything new," Wren said wearily.

"But I did!" cried Tim.

Wren gasped and her head snapped up. "You did? What?"

"You'll never believe what I just learned."

"What is it?" Wren caught his arm and shook it. "Tell me now!"

Tim looked around and lowered his voice. "Paula Gantz did take the money."

Wren fell back a step. "What? What makes you think so?"

"I don't think. I know."

Wren looked at her notebook and her heart sank. Had she gone to all this work for nothing?

12

DEDUCTIVE REASONING

Wren walked slowly to the bench and sank down beside Bess. "Tim, tell me what you know," she said in a voice just above a whisper.

Tim stood before Wren and looked very pleased with himself. A breeze ruffled his red hair and his freckles stood out boldly on his face. "I saw her just a few minutes ago hiding the money bag."

Wren leaped up. "What? What did you say?"

Tim nodded. "That's right. She had it in her hand and she pushed it under a bush beside her garage."

"But why would she do that?" Wren wrung her cold hands.

"To keep us from learning the truth, I guess. How should I know?"

"I know," said Bess.

Wren turned on her with an impatient frown.

"Don't be mad at me, Wren House!" Bess pulled herself up and looked Wren right in the eye. "I'm not the one who hid the bag. I'm not the one who took the money."

Wren threw up her hands. "Bess!"

"Tell us what you know," said Tim.

"And tell it fast!" cried Wren.

Bess looked hurt. "I know that Paula didn't want you to know that the money bag suddenly appeared on her steps. She was afraid it would look suspicious, so she hid it. She didn't want anyone but me to know." Bess shot a look at Tim. "Especially not people who already think she's guilty."

"Like you, Tim Avery!" cried Paula, leaping into sight and pointing at Tim.

Wren ran to Paula and grabbed her arm. "Tell me about the money bag!"

Paula peeled Wren's fingers loose. "Bess already told you."

"I want every detail! Every single detail! How could you keep important evidence from me?"

"How was I to know you wouldn't close the case and say I was guilty?"

"Aren't you?" asked Tim, his eyes narrowed.

"No!" Wren picked at the edge of her jacket. "I think it's a good time to do some deductive reasoning."

"I think you're right," said Tim.

"I think it's time to solve the case!" cried Paula, almost in tears.

"Who put the money bag on your step?" asked Bess.

"I don't know!"

Wren opened her notebook. "I think we'd better go over and over the case of the missing money. Every detail."

Paula sank to the edge of the bench. "How will that help?"

Wren sat on the picnic table and opened the book on her lap. She pulled the stub of a pencil from her jacket pocket. "Now then, let me see."

Paula scooted over beside Wren and peered down at the notebook. "You've been over this a lot of times, Wren."

"I know, but we'll go over it again." Wren narrowed her eyes thoughtfully. "Let me see. You had the money in your possession for a very short time Tuesday morning just after you arrived at school."

"Right."

"So you say," muttered Tim.

Wren frowned at him and he clamped his mouth closed. She looked back at Paula. "You checked it out of the office."

"Yes."

"What good is all this?" asked Bess.

"You walked right into class with the bag."

"Yes. I told you that a million times already!"

"You stuck it inside Miss Brewster's drawer."

"Right."

"And then it was gone."

"Yes." Paula threw up her arms. "Yes! Yes! I've told you over and over and over!"

"I know." Wren glanced at her scribbling. She couldn't read some of the words, but she could make a guess. "Who did you talk to inside the office?"

"Miss Radcliff."

"Did she give you the money bag?"

"Yes. It was in the lockbox in her desk."

"Fine." Wren tapped her pencil against the notebook. "Who did you talk to in the hallway before you reached your desk?"

"Nobody."

"Nobody?"

"That's right."

"While the bag was in your hands in the classroom, who did you talk to?"

"Nobody."

Wren scratched an itch on her leg. She should've gone inside to change into play clothes, but too much was happening. "Are you sure you didn't speak to anyone?"

"I might've said hello, but I didn't stop and talk to anyone."

"You'd better find out who put the empty bag on your step," said Tim.

Paula turned on him with a squeal. "Do you finally

believe someone else put the bag there?"

Tim shrugged his shoulders. "I might."

"You do, Tim," said Wren. "I never work for a client that I think is guilty."

"I'm going home," said Bess. "I'm tired of sitting here getting my hair blown all over." She waited for an objection, but didn't hear any, so she shrugged and walked to her house.

"About the bag on the step," said Tim, "Paula, was it there when you got home?"

"Yes."

"How do you know it was the same bag?" asked Wren.

"It had my initials on the inside where I'd written them," said Paula. "It was my money bag all right."

"Did anyone give you money for the bag Tuesday morning?" asked Wren.

"No." Paula gasped. "Yes!"

Wren's heart leaped. "Who?"

"Kris. Kris Bower had three checks for me. She gave them to me and I marked them on the paper and dropped them in the bag."

Wren flipped through her notebook. "I don't have that down. You didn't tell me about Kris before."

"Kris had three checks and she gave them to me, and then I gave the bag to Miss Brewster, and she put it in the second drawer of the desk." Paula was trembling with excitement. "Kris saw me give the bag to Miss Brewster."

Paula grabbed Wren's notebook. "Did you question her?"

"Hey!" Wren grabbed the notebook back and rubbed it lovingly. "This is for my hands only."

"Did you question Kris?"

"Kris wasn't in school yesterday or the day before," said Tim.

"That's right!" cried Wren. "I have that down. See?" She thumped the page that was marked KRIS BOWER.

Paula shook her head hard. "No! She was there! She did give me three checks. I put them in my bag!"

"You must have your days confused," said Wren. "That's easy enough to do. She probably handed you the money on Monday morning."

Paula wrinkled her face in thought. "Was it Monday morning? But it seemed like Tuesday."

"I think you should call Kris," said Tim.

"Good idea. I tried to talk to her this morning, but she went home before I could."

"How come you didn't go to her house and talk to her?" Paula jumped off the table and stood on the grass with her fists doubled at her sides and her chest heaving. "You're supposed to follow every lead!"

"Wren's a good detective," said Tim. "She'll talk to Kris."

Wren smiled at Tim.

"That's right." Just then a picture of Kris standing in the hallway that morning flashed in Wren's mind. Kris had been wearing a red skirt that she wore often and a black and red blouse with a black sweater vest over it. Another picture flashed in her mind—the snapshot of Kris that Brian had shown her. Kris had been walking out the door and she'd been dressed in different clothes. The photo had been black and white, but Wren knew the skirt that Kris had been wearing. It was a pink and gray plaid skirt and she wore a pink sweater with it.

"What's wrong, Wren?" asked Tim.

"I think Paula is right."

"Of course I'm right," said Paula. "About what?"

"Tuesday and Kris."

"I knew it!" Paula clapped her hands together.

"What did you remember, Wren?" asked Tim. "This is very serious, and you know you can't accuse Kris of being guilty if she isn't."

Paula jabbed a finger at Tim. "You accused me of being guilty and I wasn't."

Tim flushed. "Sorry."

Wren quickly told them about Brian's snapshot. She was too excited about the case to quiver over his name.

Paula flung out her arms. "You should've questioned her already! What kind of detective are you?"

Wren pressed her lips tightly together. She wouldn't argue with Paula. She had to keep her mind clear and alert. She was on to something and she had to follow it through. Once again she flipped through the notebook.

"I made a note that Kris was absent Tuesday, yesterday, and today."

"But she was in school at least a few minutes of all three days," said Tim.

"She gave me three checks, and she watched me hand the bag to Miss Brewster. I didn't make that up. She was there!"

"You're right," said Wren.

"She's the one that put the empty bag on my step!" cried Paula.

"Maybe," said Wren.

Paula doubled her fists and poked out her chin. "I did not make that up, Wren House!"

"I'm sure you didn't."

Paula relaxed slightly. "Do you think Kris took the money?"

"I think she did."

Paula scrambled back onto the table. "Why would she do it?"

"I don't know. Let's do a little more deductive reasoning."

"How do we start?"

"We already know Kris had opportunity," said Tim as he sat beside Wren at the table. "Now we have to find a motive."

"A motive?" asked Paula. "What's that, and why bother?"

"A motive is a reason for doing something and we need to find one because we don't know beyond a shadow of a doubt that she's guilty," said Tim.

Wren smiled at him and he grinned back. "I'll name off a list of motives and we'll see if any of them fit Kris." Wren flipped to the back of her book where she had her list. For a minute she remembered the day last year that Dad had helped her make up the list of motives. It had been one of her best days ever. Dad had treated her as if she was a real detective just like he was. She'd printed the list carefully on a lined piece of paper. It was one of her most prized possessions, and she kept it between two pieces of cardboard in a special place in her desk. She copied it carefully inside each new spiral notebook and then returned the original list to its hiding place.

Paula ran a finger around the neck of her sweater. "Well?"

"Read it," said Tim.

Wren looked intently at the first word.

13

THE LIST

Wren glanced at Tim and Paula, then looked back down at her list with pride and read the first word. "Envy."

Paula nodded. "Yes. Envy for sure! Kris wanted the job of keeping the list and the money."

"Who said?" asked Tim.

"She did," said Paula, looking at Tim as if to dare him not to believe her. "She told me she should get to do it and not me because she had attended JCA longer than I have."

Tim nodded. "Okay."

"Lust," said Wren.

"Lust?" Paula frowned.

"I guess not." Wren slid her finger down the list. "Hatred."

Paula wrinkled her nose. "Kris doesn't like me much."

Wren could name several people who didn't like Paula, but she didn't say so. "Malice?"

"I don't even know that word, Wren."

"I don't either," said Tim.

Wren kind of knew, but she couldn't find the right words to define it so she went on. "Greed."

"No," said Tim.

"Financial need."

"Kris attends JCA," said Paula. "She can't be poor."

"Right," said Tim.

"Revenge."

Paula shook her head. "Revenge? What have I done to her?"

Wren waved the short pencil. "Kris could want revenge. But how about 'irresistible impulse'? That means she wanted the money and couldn't stop herself from taking it."

"No. That's dumb."

"I agree," said Tim, leaning over to peer down at Wren's list.

"Playing a trick." Wren frowned thoughtfully. Most of the boys in the fifth grade loved to play tricks. "Several people would've had that motive."

"Not Kris," said Tim.

"You're right. Causing embarrassment."

"Yes!!" cried Paula, shaking her head.

"You're right. Retribution."

"What's that?"

Wren tried to remember and couldn't. "That's not her motive."

"What else?" asked Tim.

"That's it. But from the list we've picked out envy, revenge, causing embarrassment to Paula, and possible hatred. Now we know Kris had opportunity and motive."

"Opportunity and motive," said Tim with a grin.

"What's so funny?" asked Paula sharply.

"Nothing," said Tim, but Wren knew and laughed under her breath. Detective talk had a beauty all its own.

Paula slapped her legs. "She did it all right! That terrible girl! How could she do that to me? She'll sure be sorry."

Wren touched the list with the tips of her fingers. "We don't know beyond a shadow of doubt that she is guilty, Paula."

"I know!" cried Paula.

"No, you don't," said Tim.

"I do!"

Wren shook her finger at Paula. "I don't, and you hired me to solve the case."

Paula jumped up and stood with her fists on her hips. "You're off the case now. I'll take it from here."

Wren closed her notebook and jabbed the pencil through the spiral. "You can't take me off the case. Not now. I'm going to see this to the end. That's the way I work."

"That's right," said Tim. "You hired the best person for the case, and you can't fire her just when she's ready to close the case."

A special warmth wrapped around Wren's heart, and she couldn't believe that she'd ever hated Tim Avery. He was special, and she was thankful that God had helped her to learn it.

Paula sighed and pushed her hair back. "All right. All right! You're hired back."

Wren tucked her dark hair behind her ears. "I have to find out if she did take the money!"

Paula drooped. "But how? If she did take it, she sure wouldn't tell us if we asked."

Wren opened and closed her notebook and ran her hand over it. Finally she looked up. "You're right about that. We'll have to think of something. Something brilliant."

Tim nodded. "It really is strange that Kris put the money bag on the step. Unless she was trying to make sure you got blamed."

"She might be scared or even sorry for what she did," said Wren.

Paula wrinkled her nose. "It won't do any good for her to be sorry. I'm going to make it so hard on her, she won't ever forget that she tried to hurt me. And I won't let anyone forget that she's a thief! Let's go see her right now!"

Wren and Tim looked at each other, then turned back to Paula. "You can't go, Paula," said Wren.

"You'd scare her too much," said Tim.

"I don't care! I'm going to her house and punch her lights out!" Paula danced around, jabbing the air with her fists. "I'll smash her face in! I'll make her sorry she ever took that money!"

Wren caught Paula's arm and pulled her up short. "You will not do any of those things, Paula Gantz!"

"Who says?"

"We say!" cried Tim, his eyes flashing and his chin set determinedly.

"She deserves to be hurt," snapped Paula.

Wren shook her head. "Have you forgotten the parable of the unmerciful servant from Matthew 18 that Miss Brewster read to us yesterday?"

Paula frowned. "What about it?"

"I remember," said Tim excitedly. "A servant owed the king lots of money, and the king was going to toss the servant and his wife and children into jail until the debt was paid."

"This is dumb," said Paula, but she stood and listened anyway.

"The servant begged the king to be patient with him," said Wren. "The servant said he'd pay back everything."

"So the king canceled the debt, and the servant was free," Tim said.

"Is this true?" asked Paula, looking doubtful.

"It's a story that Jesus told to teach a lesson on forgiveness," said Wren. "But there's more."

"I don't want to listen! I want to find Kris and sock her in the face!" Paula swung her fist, and once again Wren caught her arm.

"Stop it, Paula!" cried Wren. "And listen!"

Tim stabbed his fingers through his red hair. "The servant was glad he wasn't going to jail. Outside he saw a fellow servant that owed him a few dollars."

"The servant grabbed his fellow servant by the throat!" Wren grabbed Paula's jacket at her throat and shook it. "He said, 'Listen, fellow servant, you owe me a few dollars and you'll pay me back now! If you don't, I am going to toss you and your family in prison until the debt is paid!' The fellow servant begged to be given a few more days to pay the debt. But the servant wouldn't give him a few more days, and had him thrown into prison."

"But that's terrible!" cried Paula.

"That's not the end," said Tim. "The king learned what the servant had done. He called the servant to him and said, 'You wicked servant! I canceled your debts and didn't toss you and your family into prison. Why didn't you show mercy to your fellow servant just as I showed mercy to you? Because you didn't, you are going to jail until your debt is paid.'"

Tim shook a finger at Paula. "Jesus wants us to forgive each other."

Wren nodded, "Remember that I forgave you even though you'd done a terrible thing to me? When we ask

Him to, God forgives us. And we're supposed to forgive others." Wren stepped right up to Paula. "You need to forgive Kris."

"No. No!" Paula shook her head hard. "I won't! I can't"

"You don't have a choice," said Tim. "Jesus says you have to forgive."

"That's true," said Wren. "You have to. We have to, too."

Paula bit her bottom lip and looked down at the grass. Finally she looked up. "I can't do it," she whispered. "I don't know how."

"Do you want to know?" asked Tim. Paula nodded.

Smiling, Wren motioned to the picnic table. "Let's sit down and talk, and then we'll go see Kris."

"Do we have to talk about this now?" asked Paula.

"Yes," said Wren and Tim together.

"It's time you decided if you want to accept Jesus as your personal Savior," said Wren.

To Wren's surprise Paula burst into tears. Paula dropped to the bench and covered her face with her hands. "I can't accept Him. I've tried and I don't know how!"

"We'll tell you how," said Tim. Wren touched Paula's hand. "Jesus loves you. He wants the very best for you." Wren smiled. "He helped me to take your case when I didn't want to."

"I know," whispered Paula. "I couldn't understand that."

"You just have to tell Jesus that you want Him as your Savior and friend," said Tim. "It's simple. You talk to Him and the Holy Spirit comes to live in your life, and He creates a new spirit inside of you."

"I don't understand," said Paula with a frown.

"You don't need to," said Wren. "You've heard us talk about faith in church and at school. This is where faith comes in. By faith you accept that Jesus is God's Son, that He rose from the dead, and that He loves you."

"The moment you ask Jesus to be your Savior and ask Him to forgive your sins, He answers," Tim added. "If you really mean it."

"And He really does make a new Paula— even if you don't feel anything," said Wren. "Jesus loves you and He wants you to love Him."

Paula sniffed and rubbed her hand across her nose. She closed her eyes. "I'm going to pray right now."

"Good," said Wren as Tim nodded.

"Jesus, I believe in You and I want You to be my Savior. Please forgive me and come live in my heart. I will live for You and do what You want me to do. I'll even forgive Kris if I have to."

Wren's heart leapt and she glanced at Tim. God had answered once again.

14

A NEW PAULA

Wren looked at Paula and smiled. "You're a new Paula."

Paula beamed. "Yes, I am!"

Tim grinned from ear to ear. "Now we can go see Kris and get this whole thing settled. But remember that we still don't know for sure that she's guilty."

"I know," said Paula grimly, then she chuckled. "I won't punch her or anything."

"Let's go," said Wren. She had a hard job ahead of her. It wasn't easy to come to the end of a case and realize she had to expose a friend. Silently she prayed for the right words to say to Kris. "I know where she lives. It won't take long to get there. I'll tell Neil where we're going. You'd better let me do the talking. Okay, Paula?"

Paula lifted her head. "Why should you get to have all the fun?"

"Paula, it's not fun to tell a friend that we think she took the money," said Tim.

"I know," whispered Paula. "It's just that I don't want to keep my mouth closed all the time."

"You don't want to frighten Kris, do you?" Wren asked.

"I guess not." Paula sighed. "I just want the money returned and my name cleared."

A few minutes later Wren pedaled down the street with Tim and Paula close behind. The sun shone brightly and sparkled off the few puddles left from the rain. She stopped at a street crossing, waited for traffic, then rode across.

Outside Kris's house Wren said, "Wait, Paula. Remember that we don't know that Kris took the money. We can't leap on her and demand it back. We have to be very careful."

Paula stood with her hands on her waist and a determined look on her face. "Well, I know she took it!"

"We don't know for sure. Do we? Do we, Paula?" Wren waited until Paula gave a reluctant shake of her head. "We're going to be nice to Kris. If she really did take the money, I know she'll be feeling very guilty about it. We want to give her a chance to admit she took it, if she really did."

Paula rolled her eyes. "You think you know everything, don't you?"

"Almost everything." Tim grinned, and the tension eased.

They laid their bikes on the grass beside the front walk

and Wren rang the doorbell. Shivers of excitement ran up and down her back. A few butterflies fluttered in her stomach. Maybe the case would end and Dad wouldn't have to step in and solve it.

Mrs. Bower opened the door and looked surprised. Smells of fried chicken and freshly baked bread drifted from the kitchen. "Hello. Wren, isn't it? And Tim and Paula?"

Wren nodded.

"We came to talk to Kris," said Paula.

"Well, I don't know." Mrs. Bower glanced behind her. "She hasn't been feeling well and she spent the day in her room."

"We won't stay long," said Tim.

Mrs. Bower stepped aside. "All right. Come in. Her room is just down the hallway, the third door on the right."

A few seconds later Paula knocked on the door and when Kris answered, the girls said, "Hi."

"We'd like to talk to you," said Tim.

The color drained from Kris's face. "I'm not feeling well."

"We'll cheer you up," said Wren.

"We sure will," muttered Paula, then closed her mouth at a look from Wren.

"You don't have to be frightened," said Tim.

Kris held the door wide. "Who says I'm afraid? Come

in. My room's a mess."

"It doesn't matter," said Wren.

Kris took their jackets and draped them over a chair near her closet. Clothes were piled in a heap at the foot of the bed. Books and papers were strewn across the floor. Kris turned to face her visitors, but didn't speak. Nervously she rubbed her hands down the legs of her jeans and twisted her foot on the carpet.

Wren stood beside Kris's unmade bed. "We came to talk about something important."

"Something very important," said Paula. She looked grim and Wren frowned at her.

Kris looked from one to the other and began to tremble. She touched her tangled hair and picked at the bottom of her sweater.

Wren stood with her hands at her sides, her feet apart. "Kris, Tuesday you gave Paula three checks from people who paid for newspaper subscriptions."

"That's right." With quick, jerky movements Kris pushed her long hair back. Tension filled the room.

Wren tugged her sweater down over her skirt. "Miss Brewster says that you weren't in school Tuesday. She marked you absent. Yesterday and today, too."

"I was absent." Kris moved restlessly.

"But I saw you this morning, so I know you were there," said Wren softly. She could tell just by looking at Kris that she was guilty. Wren wanted to feel glad the case was solved, but she felt too sorry for Kris to feel any triumph.

"And we know you were there Tuesday morning," said Tim.

"You have something to tell us, don't you?" asked Paula sharply.

"No!" Kris backed away.

"Yes, you do," said Wren. She wanted to say more, but she didn't. She wanted to give Kris a fair chance to tell her story.

Kris rubbed a trembling hand over her face. "What're you trying to do to me? I got sick and I had to come home! Ask my mom!"

"Do you want to tell us about the bag of money?" asked Wren softly.

Kris's face crumpled as she looked from one to the other. "I don't know what . . . what you're talking . . . about."

Paula frowned, but didn't speak.

"We think you took the money," said Tim. "And we think you were sorry about doing it, but you put the empty bag on Paula's step with hopes that she'd be forced to take the blame."

"That's dumb!" Tears sparkled in Kris's eyes.

Wren walked to the single bed and sank to the edge. She picked up a stuffed bear and hugged it close. "Kris, we're pretty sure of what we're talking about. You had opportunity to take the bag of money and you had reason."

"That's right," said Tim. "Opportunity and motive."

"I know you wanted to make me look bad in front of the class," said Paula. "It worked. I don't think I have a single friend left at school. Isn't that what you wanted?"

Kris pressed her hands to her burning cheeks. "No! Well, maybe." She turned to Wren. "I didn't intend to take it. I was going to hide it and have someone find it and let everyone think Paula had done it. But I saw the bag of money, and I took it and walked right out of the school before I really knew what I was doing. And once it was done, I was afraid to say anything." Kris hung her head. "I've been trying to find a way to tell Miss Brewster. But I'm not brave. I'm a coward."

"So you're admitting to it," whispered Paula, sinking onto a chair near the window.

"Yes." Kris locked her hands together in front of her. "I'm sorry!"

"We knew you would be," said Wren. "You usually don't do anything bad."

"I just couldn't help myself!" cried Kris. "I've begged God to forgive me, and I know He will now." She turned to Paula. "Will you please forgive me, Paula? I know I shouldn't have done that to you. It was wrong."

"Yes, it was," said Paula.

"Will you forgive me, Paula?"

Kris sounded close to tears. Wren sat very still and waited. It was all up to Paula now.

Tim leaned against the back of the chair with the jackets and watched Paula. Paula opened her mouth, closed it and opened it again. "I can't!" She looked helplessly at Wren.

"You can," whispered Wren. "Remember that you're not alone any longer."

"I don't deserve to be forgiven," said Kris, her eyes fixed on the floor.

Paula took a deep breath and locked her hands in front of her. "Kris, I . . . I forgive you. I do forgive you!" The words rushed out of her as if she'd had to say them fast before she changed her mind.

A smile broke across Kris's face and lit up the whole room. "Thank you, Paula!"

Wren jumped up with a smile. "Good going, Paula!"

"Way to go, Paula," said Tim.

Paula stood straight and looked very proud of herself.

Wren turned to Kris. "Where's the money, Kris?"

Kris slowly picked up her pillow and reached inside the case. She pulled out the bills and checks held together with a rubber band and handed them to Paula. "Here's the money. You can take it now or I can return it in the morning and tell Miss Brewster what I did."

"I'll take it," said Paula. She looked at the money, then hugged it to her fiercely. "I wasn't guilty! See? I wasn't!"

Wren and Tim smiled at Paula, then at each other.

"Great job, Wren," mouthed Tim.

Wren beamed. "Thanks for helping," she whispered back.

"Anytime."

"I'll tell Miss Brewster," said Kris. "I don't know how, but I'll tell her. Maybe I'll call her tonight."

"Good," said Paula. Wren held out her hand to Kris. "Remember that God is with you to help you talk to Miss Brewster."

Kris nodded. "That's right. He is. He loves me."

"And He loves me," whispered Paula in awe.

Wren blinked back tears as joy burst inside her and she laughed aloud.

With sparkling eyes Paula turned to Wren. "The case is closed, Wren."

"It sure is!" Wren headed for the door, eager to find another mystery to solve.

Adam Straight to the Rescue

Ketchup on pancakes?

Adam has always wanted brothers and sisters . . . but this ready-made family isn't quite what he had in mind. Three-year-old Jory is cute enough, although his fascination with meat-eating dinosaurs can get out of hand. But ten-year-old Belinda is another story. How can Adam put up with a sister who calls his mother E. S. (short for Evil Stepmother), makes up stories just to scare him, and eats ketchup on everything?

"When we get back from our camping trip," his mom assures him, "it'll seem like we've been together forever." Adam's not so sure, although the two-day trip packs enough adventure to last most families a lifetime. And in spite of—or maybe because of—runaway cars, midnight animal visitors, and trips to the emergency room, Adam does some serious thinking and praying about what it means to be a brother. As he says, "I don't know why I argue with You, God. It's hard work. And besides, You always win!"

K.R. Hamilton lives with her husband and kids in Birmingham, Alabama. She has worked as a ranch hand, a lumberjack, a census taker, and an archeological surveyor, among other things. She's not likely to run out of things to write about.

Adam Straight and the Mysterious Neighbor

Listen to the "Spider Lady"?

Adam isn't sure he wants to do yardwork for Miss Winters. She lives in a run-down old house on an overgrown lot, doesn't want him knocking on the door, and warns him to stay out of the fenced-in backyard. And now a strange man in a black suit calls her the Spider Lady! Something creepy is going on here.

But Adam needs the money, thanks to his stepsister Belinda's latest successful attempt to get him into trouble. And working with his new friend, Pelican, will be fun. But before Adam even realizes how it happened, he's become something of a spider himself—spinning a web of half-truths and misunderstandings that make Belinda even angrier and may cost him Pelican's friendship.

Before the mystery is solved, Adam finds that he and Belinda aren't so different after all . . . and that God's forgiveness is something a Christian needs—and can count on—time and time again.

K. R. Hamilton lives with her husband and kids in Birmingham, Alabama. She has worked as a ranch hand, a lumberjack, a census taker, and an archeological surveyor, among other things. She's not likely to run out of things to write about.

The Best Defense

"You sure know how to make a mother worry."

Josh has lived in Grandville barely two months, and he's already met the paramedics, the police, some teenaged would-be thugs, and a long-haired leather worker named Sonny. No wonder his mom gets a little anxious from time to time.

Josh thinks karate lessons would take care of some of his worries, but they aren't likely to help his relationship with Samantha Sullivan, the bossiest kid in the fifth grade. And they won't make his dad call more often.

Sonny tells him the key to conquering his fear is prayer . . . but Josh isn't sure that prayer is the answer. He needs to explore the possiblility. What if it doesn't work in a dark tunnel when he's facing two thugs?

ELAINE K. McEWAN, an elementary school principal and the mother of two grown children, knows a lot of kids like Josh.

Project Cockroach

"We'll go down in Jefferson School history."

That's what Ben Anderson promises when he gets Josh to agree to his plan. And turning loose a horde of cockroaches in Mrs. Bannister's desk drawer does sound impressive. Josh knows what Wendell, his peculiar next-door neighboor and classmate, would say, but what would you expect from a kid who actually goes to the library in the summertime?

Josh's mom wants him to be a good student and stay out of trouble. His long-distance dad back in Woodview wants him to "have a good year." Wendell wants him to go to church. But Josh isn't sure that even God can help him find answers to the questions in his life. He just wants to make a few friends and fit into his new world . . . even if it means taking a risk or two.

ELAINE K. McEWAN, an elementary school principal and the mother of two grown children, knows a lot of kids like Josh.